To Sarah
I hope [you enjoy]
 reading

A TROUBLED SOUL

A Willow Green Village Cozy Mystery

Evelyn Harrison

Warmest wishes
Evelyn Harrison
7.7.2015

Raven Crest Books

Copyright © 2015 Evelyn Harrison

The right of Evelyn Harrison to be identified as the author of this work has been asserted by her in accordance with the Copyright, Designs and Patents Act 1988

All rights reserved.

This is a work of fiction. Names, characters, businesses, places, events and incidents are either the products of the author's imagination or used in a fictitious manner. Any resemblance to actual persons, living or dead, or actual events is purely coincidental.

No part of this publication may be reproduced, stored in a retrieval system or transmitted in any form or by any means including photocopying, electronic, recording or otherwise, without the prior written permission of the rights holder, application for which must be made through the publisher.

Cover Design by www.StunningBookCovers.com

ISBN-13: 978-0-9931909-8-8
ISBN-10: 0-99-319098-7

Writing can be a very lonely business and it helps to have an encouraging circle of family and friends around you. So this is my time to say thank you, to those wonderful folk. First of all to my family for their continued support, with special mention to my daughter, Sarah. Second my friends, Lorraine, Nikki, Claire and in particular Sally, for their endless patience. Thank you, each and every one of you.

CHAPTER 1 – I REMEMBER

Some people will tell you they can remember when they were four years old – perhaps playing in the sand at the seaside with a large red bucket and spade – whereas, in fact, they had been told the story of their first beach holiday by their adoring parents. They even ignore the reality that they have seen the photos of this blissful time in the lovingly produced family album – still insisting they remembered.

I, on the other hand, definitely remember being four. For it was on my fourth birthday I first saw the vision – the sad face of a woman, enveloped in a shimmering grey vapour – following a curious compulsion to gaze up towards my bedroom window from our sprawling garden below. Surprisingly, it had not scared me, seeing the ashen face looking down upon me, as I played with my two little friends – in a strange way, for once in my short life, I felt comforted.

Just as my eyes alighted on my bedroom window, a rough hand had unexpectedly lifted me off my feet and dragged me indoors in order for me to blow out the four pink candles twinkling in the dimly lit kitchen of Hill Farm. Hill Farm, which stood majestically on the highest point at the edge of Willow Green village, was my home and my private hell.

I really did not want them to leave – my two little friends, who I watched run eagerly towards the open arms of their doting mothers. It was with reluctance that I waved to them as they drove steadily away down the stony drive fear in me building as to the possible punishment awaiting me.

"You wicked girl!" my own mother screamed, slapping my bare, spindly legs, which appeared bruised and pale below my new red velvet dress. "Take it off before you get anything else down it. Take it off! Are you deaf as well as stupid?"

Trying to hold back the tears now streaming down my colourless cheeks, I stepped out of the beautiful dress I had been so proud to wear. A large muddy stain had dried hard down one side, embedding itself into the once gorgeously soft material, the result of my fall into my mother's pride and joy, a sizeable bed of bluebells. I was not completely sure if she was angry with me for dirtying my dress, or the annihilation of half the bed of vivid blue flowers that normally stood swaying under the dappled shade beneath the deciduous trees at the side of the house – but angry she certainly was.

"Bed, now!" she bellowed, "don't even think about your dad coming to say goodnight to you when he comes in. You wicked, wicked girl!" she repeated, spitting out the words, as her face contorted with rage.

I crawled under my green woollen blanket, pulling it up over my head. Although it was a very warm evening and I was already hot and sticky, I truly believed if I covered my entire body I could disappear – become invisible. My nana's voice from the room below reached up through the knurled floorboards, pleading my case.

"I'm sure it was an accident Rosemary she seemed so pleased with the dress and dear, it is the 1980s not the 1880s, you do have a washing machine."

"Don't mum, just don't, ok?"

From the nursery along the landing, I could hear my baby brother's sudden, urgent call for attention – the yell that came from his lungs was always intense but had an amazingly calming effect on my mother. Her tone always seemed to mellow rapidly when she spoke to him, a sort of soothing, cooing sound I had never been privy to. What had I done, for her to hate me so much?

The air around my room began to cool as my eyes closed to the world around me and I drifted thankfully into the world of dreams. The unrecognisable face of the woman I had seen appeared to me that night. It was as if she had swept me up into her arms, holding me tenderly, not wanting to let me go — it was a wonderful, peaceful feeling of complete contentment, so much so, I did not want to wake up.

CHAPTER 2 – A GERMAN INVASION

Wake up I did, of course, with the sun streaming through the gap in my floral curtains, poignantly illuminating the picture of Jesus that hung on the opposite wall, his head tilting tenderly towards me, the expression on his saintly face exuding love. Rubbing my eyes, I wearily eased myself down from my bed, leaving my room to join the rest of the family already at the breakfast table. My little brother, Ben, was doing his usual trick of throwing the contents of his cereal bowl all over the floor.

"Morning, sleepyhead," chirped Nana Western as she set a bowl of steaming porridge before me. How I loved it when nana and grandad came to stay, for the house seemed a much happier place – well, usually it did, but it was soon apparent my mother had still not forgiven me for the previous day's debacle.

"Not dressed yet?" she roared.

"She's only four, Rosemary, you needed help with dressing until you started school," nana pointed out, coming to my aid.

"Doggie." Ben, now halfway out of his chair, threw the rest of his cereal down to the excited terrier circling below, who was enthusiastically mopping up the food from the grossly stained carpet.

"Come on Katy, I'll help you find some outdoor clothes, Penny needs a walk." Penny, nana's little black Cairn terrier, was a bundle of joy with her stubby wagging tail and small attentive ears.

Out in the morning sunshine, holding my nana's hand tightly, I looked up into her kind, wrinkled face; how I wished she and grandad lived with us all the time. We walked slowly up the steep dirt track weaving its way towards the six-barred gate of the first orchard full of apple trees where my father was already busy aboard his tractor. We waved to him as he went about his business, collecting dead branches lying beneath the tree canopies at the onset of blossom.

Penny pulled tightly on her lead, selfishly not wanting to stop as she sniffed the air excitedly, blissfully inhaling the smells of the breath-taking countryside around her. I surveyed my father with some sadness as his muddied tractor headed away from me and out of view, chugging onwards towards the next field and beyond.

All too soon, our walk was at an end and it was time for my grandparents to leave. I threw my arms around both of them, squeezing so tightly before they climbed into their car. My grandad, lighting his pipe before the long journey ahead, grunted something I did not quite hear. Watching their vehicle roll carefully down the lane, crunching loudly the loose gravel beneath its rotating wheels – I prayed under my breath they would hurry back soon.

At the dinner table that evening, mother announced right out of the blue that she needed more help in the house.

"Mrs. Devine cleans twice a week, are you saying you need her more often than that?" my father queried, as he tried to saw through the pork chop which had almost been cremated by my mother's attempt at cooking.

"What I mean, Jonathan, is I need an au pair. I listened to a programme on Radio 4 today and apparently employment agencies have been inundated with girls from various European countries who long to come to England to work and study English. All we have to do is provide accommodation and a little pocket money; in return, they look after the children."

Father looked down at his plate and began to push the remaining bone slowly around with his fork.

"Are you mad, woman? We've had enough trouble with the foreign fruit pickers we employ on the farm; why the hell would you want one living in our house?"

"I'm talking about decent girls from decent homes, who want to better themselves by getting an education, not sluts who steal husbands!"

With that, she rose from the table, slamming the door as she swept out of the room.

***

Three months later, Wilfreda arrived, her battered suitcase full to the brim with clothes. She was a particularly well-developed young woman, about twenty years old, and spoke very little English. Father seemed to change his mind instantly about the idea of having a foreigner in our house when he set eyes on her and immediately volunteered to show her around the farm.

A few days after Wilfreda's arrival, I overheard Mrs. Devine telling Miss Cain, the postmistress, when she took me into the village for a treat, how nervous she felt about having a German in close vicinity. Not that she could remember much about the war, she had added, as she had been too young, but nonetheless she was watching her back.

I did not understand what she meant at the time, but on reflection, Wilfreda was definitely not to be trusted; I am sure it was not because she was German, for I now have many German friends who are very decent human beings.

The deal was that Wilfreda was to look after Ben and me five days a week, and two days a week she would attend college to study English and Home Economics. Of course, the days Wilfreda looked after us gave our mother a timeout card, time to do her own thing, that meant her leaving the house most days and not returning until the evening meal which Wilfreda thankfully cooked.

At the beginning, everything was fine, especially when it was Mrs. Devine's day to clean. Wilfreda would play with us; something our mother never did, and read us stories (although not always appropriate, especially the paperbacks from her library of romance novels) in order to practice her English. However, as the months passed, Wilfreda became a little disgruntled with her lot; she felt put upon by mother, who was asking more and more of her. I could not help but notice she was becoming a little less interested in our welfare and more interested in flirting with the overseas workers who were now arriving in their droves.

Not only that, she was getting into the habit of not dressing herself until lunchtime; father seemed a little perplexed one day when he found her sprawled out in the lounge in just a push-up bra and French knickers. He sent Ben and me straight to our rooms so he could have a long conversation with her about her behaviour. They had several 'long conversations' over the next few weeks, usually on a Thursday, when mother was out.

One day in late September, I was aware of a repellent smell on Wilfreda's breath as she leant over to wash my hair while I was bathing. She also seemed a little unsteady on her feet and I was more than a little alarmed as she picked me up roughly and swung me around and around until, quite honestly, I felt extremely sick; so sick, in fact, that I was all down her clean clothes. She was not happy at all, screaming profanities in German as she threw me into my bedroom before shutting the door behind her.

I learnt how to dress myself that day, pulling on an old pair of trousers and a torn t-shirt from my bottom drawer, even though my right arm was throbbing painfully. Before long, Ben's loud cries from the lounge reached my ears. Cautiously, I opened my bedroom door and crept towards the stairs. My intention was to pacify my brother, and to make damn sure the monstrous Wilfreda was not hurting him as she had just hurt me.

At the top of the stairs, with joyous relief, I felt her; my spirit friend. Her presence was like a blanket of silk wrapping around me. I was not so afraid now she was letting me know she was there, giving me an inner strength to go forward to help Ben, whose cries were now so deafening I was surprised my father could not hear them out in the orchards.

There he was, lying in a heap on the floor having pulled the wooden coffee table on top of him. With all my strength, even though the pain in my arm was agonizing, I managed to push the offending item off his tormented body, but his screaming continued, reaching heights even I had not heard before. I gave him a cuddle and decided I had to find our father. Wilfreda was nowhere to be seen until, that is, I opened the door to the outhouse.

Up against the whitewashed wall, arms raised high above her head, was a half-naked Wilfreda, moaning loudly. Delicate, white lacy panties were dangling around her splayed ankles; her see-through blouse ripped open, exposing huge breasts bare for the entire world to see. Pressing powerfully against her, a dark-haired, unkempt farm worker was thrusting eagerly with his manhood – oblivious to the little girl watching. Fortunately for me, I did not understand what I was seeing, or comprehend why so much noise was erupting from these two grown-ups.

It was just at that very moment, the door to the outside world opened quietly and in stepped my father. He took a long lingering look at the spectacle being acted out in front of him, surprisingly seeming to enjoy the sight of the intercourse taking place between these two beings, that is, until he realised I was standing in the inner doorway. Erupting into a furious rage, he put an abrupt end to the pornographic scene, escorting the passionate pair from the house and away from the farm.

I never saw either of them again and for some unknown reason, as far as I know, Wilfreda was never reported to the police. Ben and I were quickly whisked away to the hospital; they found I was suffering from a badly sprained arm and Ben a broken rib. Our mother, oblivious to all the drama because our father was unable to contact her, arrived home as usual for the evening meal.

CHAPTER 3 – THE FRENCH ARE COMING

Mother was beside herself when she found out that Ben had a broken rib; she ranted and raved for several minutes about the foreigner's father allowed to work in the proximity of her child – her child!

"Mrs. Devine, would you mind taking the children up to bed please? I need to have a word with Rosemary."

Dear old Mrs. Devine had come without hesitation, when dad called her trying to find the whereabouts of mother. Gently, she helped us upstairs and into our pyjamas – kissing me goodnight, she whispered, "You're safe now, mother's home, everything will be fine."

If only that were true.

The violent argument between our parents continued into the early hours. I drifted in and out of sleep, my dreams filled with the twisted faces of Wilfreda and her over-enthusiastic lover. The following morning, father explained mother had gone to visit nana and grandad and had taken Ben with her; he added Mrs. Devine would be looking after me until she returned.

Several days later, she and Ben reappeared as if nothing had happened, and our lives resumed, but henceforth with mother paying little attention to me – which, quite honestly, I preferred to the screaming and slapping. Of course, now she was not able to enjoy her days of freedom, to which she had become accustomed, her frustrations soon began to show once more, even when it came to my precious sibling.

"Watch your brother for me, I'm just going for a quick walk, won't be long. He'll be asleep for an hour yet," she instructed me one day as she turned on my favourite cartoon.

It was strange how she spoke to me on these occasions, seeming to ignore the fact that I was a very young child myself. Who in their right mind leaves two children under five alone? A desperate woman unhappy with her life – that's who.

When, after a while, my father appeared in the house wanting to use the telephone, he was livid to find us alone. Gathering us up into his strong arms, he took us outside into the yard looking all around him for signs of his absent wife. Buckling us into his Land Rover, he turned the key, eager to start the engine, with the intention of searching the farm as fast as he could. Just then, mother strode into the yard from the lane, looking flustered and bedraggled.

"Where the fuck have you been?" father yelled. "Anything could have happened to the children!"

"Did anything happen?" she snapped, then, continuing her response before he could reply, "No, didn't think so," and marched away from us into the house without looking back.

***

Gabrielle's presence brought immediate peace and harmony into our troubled household. She was our new au pair from across the channel but, unlike Wilfreda, spoke quite good English. Strangely, I felt an instant rapport with her, as if I knew her and she knew me – she was simply wonderful and I instantly fell in love with her.

Although it was the middle of winter, every day she would wrap us warmly in our coats and scarves and guide us along the frosty lanes, bringing much-needed colour to our pallid cheeks. Occasionally, we would catch the bus into the village, where Gabrielle would chat to the locals in her broken English. Many of the villagers were intrigued about her life and asked questions about France and being an au pair. Particularly interested was Mrs. Barbara Hamilton, who resided in the large, ivy covered Manor House which nestled comfortably near the village green.

"I have had several au pairs," she began one day when she stopped us in the street, "but none of them turned out to be 'nice girls'. If ever you want a change, Gabrielle, here is my number, please give me a ring. You would have your own wing of the house and every weekend off."

Gabrielle smiled politely as she squeezed my hand gently. "Thank you, Mrs. Hamilton, but I could never leave Katy."

My favourite time with Gabrielle was at the end of the day, when we were completely alone. During these special moments, she would hold me close and sing to me in French, her soft, angelic voice sending me into a deep, tranquil sleep that I had not been familiar with before – life was now perfect.

Gabrielle was not the only new employee in our lives at that time; Jack Palmer had been taken on as father's right-hand man to help him run the expanding farm. From what I could gather, he was an old friend of mother's who had fallen on hard times.

Uncle Jack (for that was how mother instructed us to address him) was given the use of the little tied cottage which had stood derelict for years on the far side of the lane. Mother spent several weeks helping him to clean and decorate Farm Cottage, making the space liveable for this giant of a man who seemed to put a sparkle in her eyes – although I am positive my father was oblivious to this attraction.

Easter arrived with cold winds from the north sweeping the country – the leaves of the bluebells were only just beginning to emerge from their winter bed.

"Can't believe it's her fifth birthday already," Mrs. Devine remarked, busying herself in our kitchen making sandwiches for my birthday tea.

Nana agreed. "Not only that, but she starts school next week. You are getting a big girl," she pointed out, as she lifted me high in the air.

"Put her down, mum, you'll hurt your back. Gabrielle, take Katy please and dress her in her party clothes and for god's sake do something with her hair, it looks like rats tails."

Perched on my bed in my new clothes, Gabrielle brushed my thick, black, wavy hair gently, before weaving it into my first French plait.

"There ma petite, you look beautiful." No one had ever told me I was beautiful before – as I gazed into her eyes I wished she were my mother. "Katy, I would like to give you a birthday present, something which means so much to me." She disappeared into her bedroom and returned seconds later clutching a small white box. "It was my sister's, I would so much like you to have it." I stared at the box – whose lid was decorated with a simple gold design – and thought it the most wonderful present anyone had ever given me.

On its side sat a tiny key, just waiting to be wound. Turning it carefully, Gabrielle remarked eagerly, "Lift the lid, Katy."

I lifted the lid and squealed with delight at the sight of a tiny ballerina, at the heart of the pale pink velvet interior, revolving slowly to the fairy-like music in this magical jewellery box.

"Oh thank you, Gabrielle, I love it, I will keep it forever."

Obviously delighted at my reaction, Gabrielle continued to speak tenderly, as she removed a necklace from around her neck. "I have had this locket since I was little like you, I wear it all the time," carefully, she opened the silver heart. "This is a photo of my sister Alita; whose box I have just given you and look on the other side I have put a picture of you." I was thrilled. "Ma petite, would you like to visit France one day? I would very much like to show you."

"Yes, Gabrielle. Oh yes, please." With that, she hugged me tightly and for the first time, I felt truly loved.

***

My first day of school dawned, mother giving some lame excuse for not being able to take me, so it was Gabrielle who held my hand through the imposing school gates, before my teacher escorted me into my classroom. I was very relieved to find Beth Forrester, one of the little girls from my birthday party, settling down on the mat beside me, as we began our new journey together.

The weeks passed blissfully, going to school and being looked after by Gabrielle. At the weekends we still had our walks along the lanes, but now the hedgerows and fruit trees were full of blossom and the fields carpeted with vibrant wild flowers.

On one particular Saturday, we started our walk a bit later than usual, as an unpredicted thunderstorm and torrential rain meant we'd had to wait until after lunch. Mother had already left the house, for I had watched her from the window walking across the yard towards Uncle Jack's cottage; I remember thinking she must be returning his clean washing, a task she had undertaken, because he did not have a washing machine. In reality, Mrs. Devine did the washing, but mother took the credit.

Anyway, on the way back from our walk, for some reason I ran off. Passing Farm Cottage, I thought I heard mother's voice. Standing on tiptoes upon an upturned bucket, I tried to peer through the window of the grey stone building, to see if I could see her, but the window was just too high.

"Katy, what are you doing? Why did you run off like that?" puffed Gabrielle as she arrived beside me. "Get down like a good girl."

"Mother, mother's in there," I pointed out to her. Gabrielle looked gingerly into the room and was immediately shaken at the sight that met her eyes. There she was, my mother, lying naked on the floor, surrounded by multi-coloured cushions, a sweaty Uncle Jack on top of her, his buttocks rising and falling, while mother's legs entwined his waist, pink-painted nails digging firmly into his back. Just as Gabrielle let out a low gasp, mother's eyes turned towards the window.

"Let's go Katy, let's run home very quickly!" Gathering Ben rapidly up in her arms, we ran to the house and closed the door hastily behind us.

***

Unexpected raised voices woke me early the following morning. Usually when I opened my eyes Gabrielle would be there waiting to help me dress before breakfast, but this particular morning she was nowhere to be seen. Halting at the top of the stairs, I could hear the elevated tone of my mother.

"She's taken the earrings you bought me for Christmas, Jonathan, I really loved them."

A voice I did not recognise interrupted her. "Is there anything else missing Mrs. Oliver, as far as you are aware of at the moment, that is?"

"Everything has been turned over, it will take me time," my mother sobbed.

Slowly, I descended the stairs until the adults came into focus. Sitting with my parents were two police officers, both writing frantically in their notebooks.

"Can I clarify her name again? Just want to make sure I have the correct spelling; foreign names can be a bit tricky," pointed out the largest of the men.

"G-a-b-r-i-e-l-l-e B-a-y-n-e," my father spelt out slowly.

Reaching the bottom step, I ran over to him. "Daddy, where's Gabrielle? I can't find her."

He glanced at mother, who looked away, blowing her reddening nose into a gradually disintegrating tissue.

"I need to speak to my daughter," he informed the

officers, before lifting me up and carrying me gently into the kitchen.

It was as if someone had reached in and pulled out my heart, I could not breathe. Jumping from my father's lap, I started to run through every room in the house, tears cascading down my cheeks as I called her name.

"Gabrielle! Gabrielle!"

I could not take in what my father had just told me – Gabrielle had gone and had stolen mother's jewellery! No, no, I did not believe it; she had promised she would never ever leave me.

"Gabrielle! Gabrielle! Don't leave me. Please come back. I love you."

CHAPTER 4 – THE LADIES BOOK CLUB

For some unexplained reason, which I was never really clear about, mother's bluebells never completely rose to their normal splendour that year; perhaps the high winds and heavy rain we experienced in April had caused them to become battered, but battered they certainly were. However, this time my conscience was clear; I knew I had nothing to do with their miserable demise.

An incident happened though, about this time, which not only disturbed me but also drove a temporary wedge between mother and nana. Harold Devine, Flo's husband, a strange man with numerous jobs including being the caretaker of the village hall, was our gardener. Seeing the devastation the weather had wreaked on mother's prized plants, he took it upon himself to dig and tidy one day in the bed containing the bluebells. Little Penny, who was visiting us at the time, thought this was a great game and started digging alongside him for all she was worth, her tiny paws becoming completely encrusted in mud.

All of a sudden, after witnessing the event from inside the house, mother appeared shouting and screaming for them to stop. She yelled hysterically at Harold that she had told him explicitly not to touch that part of the garden; the poor man seemed in complete shock at her outburst and immediately put down his spade. Unfortunately, Penny, not understanding the fuss happening around her, kept digging, until – unpredictably – mother raised her foot and kicked Penny hard, causing the treasured canine to leave the ground before coming to rest amongst the wilting leaves. Yelping loudly in distress, the little mite sprinted off towards nana who, traumatised by mother's action, swore she would never speak to her again.

***

I never got over Gabrielle leaving me; the grief I felt was absolute. She had left a cavernous, empty void within my young soul that no other being could ever fill. Every night I would turn the miniature key in order to watch the ballerina dance her graceful dance, before kissing my precious box goodnight. I kept my dowry hidden within my room, not wanting anyone else to know of its existence, as its presence was my only link to the woman who had given me so much love and I could not risk it ever being taken away from me. Her name never came up in conversation again in the house; it seemed, as far as mother was concerned, Gabrielle never existed. I now felt completely alone; even my spirit friend's manifestations had ceased – had I imagined her, desperate for someone, even someone not in this world, to care about me?

School now became my sanctuary – I cherished every minute of it. Beth, who by this time had become my best friend, was my other salvation; she would often ask me around her house for tea, where it was wonderful being subjected to a warm family atmosphere (even for a short period of time), compared with the aggression and violent behaviour I experienced at home, so much so, I never wanted the time to end. One particular Tuesday after school, Beth and I were at her home, Brook Cottage, doing our homework, when Josie, her mum, appeared with a large pitcher of lemonade and four glasses.

"Nanny will be here in a minute Beth, can you help me clear the table for tea?" Eager to help, my enthusiasm got the better of me as I clumsily knocked over the tall, green plastic pitcher, the contents of which enveloped my school clothes completely, just as Beth's nan, June Wright, appeared in the room.

I was beside myself. "I'm so sorry! I'm so sorry!" I cried, frantically trying to mop up the sticky liquid, now gushing like a waterfall from the table onto the oak floorboards.

"Accidents happen," remarked June softly, "you need to get out of those wet clothes, dear. Come upstairs, I'll find you something from Beth's room."

I could not believe how kind she was being; if this had happened at home mother would have been outraged, pulled my hair and beaten me with her shoe, which was always easiest to hand – but of course, only on areas where no one else could see.

Concerned at the intensity of my distress, June opened Beth's wardrobe. "There now, how about this one?" she remarked, holding aloft a pretty, blue and white striped dress. "I think you'll look beautiful in it."

Gabrielle was the only one who had called me beautiful before, hearing someone else saying it to me, made me feel melancholy for a brief moment. Carefully, I removed my sodden clothes. Getting down to my undergarments, June gasped. "My dear child, where did you get those bruises?"

Embarrassed by my numerous contusions, I quickly donned the little cotton dress.

"I fell …," I stuttered, "…from my bike, I keep doing it. The lanes around the farm are very stony."

However, June understood, she recognised the signs, because she had been a victim herself at the hands of her own sadistic mother. She looked deep into my eyes.

"You don't have to explain to me now. I'm here if you need someone to talk to, but please believe me when I say that no one, and I mean no one, has the right to harm another human being, do you understand?" Bringing to mind her own childhood experiences, she stressed, "Remember don't let anyone tell you it's your fault they've hurt you, because it's not."

June knowing my secret did not improve my life initially, but at least now I did not feel so alone; I knew there was someone out there I could talk to, not that I felt I could admit to anyone that my very own mother hated me so much.

***

Changing schools at eleven was hard – Beth passed the eleven-plus, joining her older sister Emma at grammar school, whereas I had to settle for the large comprehensive in the town three miles away. The majority of pupils from our primary school moved there with me; unfortunately one of them was Louise Turley, a tall, lanky, blonde individual – Mrs. Devine's neighbour on the Willow Green council estate. From the very first time I met her she had made it obvious she detested me. Up until now I had Beth to champion me – but from this moment on, I had to face this bully on my own.

At home, the relationship between my parents had finally broken down completely. The majority of the time they went their separate ways, meeting occasionally at meal times just for the benefit of Ben and me. Father would spend days away from the farm, leaving Uncle Jack in sole charge; a role he seemed to thrive on, especially when it meant he could spend more 'private time' with mother. I could not understand why she was so different when he was around – even to me, although she now had very little to do with me in every way, thank god.

While my body grew, the marks of my beatings began to mend on the outside, but the scars within would not heal until many years later. Of course, as I got older, I was more aware of my parents' behaviour, understood that mother was sleeping with Uncle Jack and that father probably had a bit on the side too. If it made our lives more harmonious then … well, then I felt I had no other course but to accept it.

***

Even though I was now well over thirteen, and Ben a year or so younger, mother insisted we had a babysitter when father was away and she wanted an evening out. Usually Mrs. Devine was only too pleased to look after us, but the next time mother approached her, she was taken aback by the response.

"I'm sorry, Mrs. Oliver, I've just joined a book club and it meets every Friday, so I can't watch the children on those evenings now," Mrs. Devine stuttered, apologising profusely.

"No problem, Flo, have your book club here. Yes, why not and you could stay over, if Harold doesn't mind of course, which means I won't have to get back from my ... my get together in town with my friends until the following day. Good idea?"

Mrs. Devine could not come up with a reason quickly enough for not accepting her proposition, so the following Friday, as mother left with Uncle Jack just before dinner (who was apparently only driving her to the station!), Mrs. Devine arrived, followed some time later by three other women from the village – books in hand.

The first to cross the threshold was Laura Cain, the postmistress, an unmarried thirty-year-old (her choice, she tells anyone who's interested), who had worked in the village post office and shop since she left school and knew, and was known to, everyone in the village. Next was Emily Stanton, the wife of the Reverend Stanton, who was also a prominent member of the Women's Institute. Lastly, to my dismay, Brenda Turley, my tormenter's mother, flounced into our house looking a little slutty in an exceptionally short mini skirt. I could not help thinking this was an unlikely gathering of individuals, who you would assume had very little in common – but I suppose literature has no boundaries.

"Can I get everyone a cup of tea?" I asked politely, vaguely intrigued as to the book that had engrossed their evenings over the past week.

"Thank you Katy, that would be very kind of you," Mrs. Devine smiled; she seemed slightly overcome by my offer as she was used to waiting on me. Then she added, "Could we have an extra mug? We are expecting a guest speaker."

I hurried into the kitchen and quickly filled a large pot, which I placed on the tray decorated with a map of the British Isles (mother's Christmas present from nana), together with a plate of assorted biscuits. Arriving back with the pretty china evenly balanced, I was slightly surprised, as I placed the tray carefully on the wooden coffee table, that a debate had not yet got underway.

"I was wondering, ladies, if you would mind me sitting in on your discussion as I'm studying literature at school and I thought listening to your feedback might help me?" I asked, trying to sound grown-up amongst these distinguished women.

A frantic glance passed between them.

"Hmm, Katy," began Emily Stanton, "the book we have been reading this week ... well, quite frankly, it's an adult book; not really something someone of your age should have access to."

"Yes, that's right," added Laura Cain, looking slightly embarrassed.

"I see, I understand, well, I'll leave you to it then," I said, smarting slightly. "Ben's already in bed, Mrs. Devine, watching a tape of one of his nature programmes, so I'll say goodnight."

I exited the room with a chorus of 'goodnights' echoing behind me. I wondered about the book these women had been reading, which had caused them such embarrassment; perhaps it was full of sex and violence, however, I was sure nothing much worse than I had been privy to first hand.

I was just drifting off to sleep when I heard a persistent ring at our front door and Mrs. Devine's voice greeting their guest.

"Mrs. King, you found us, I'm sorry about the change of venue, please come in."

A couple of hours later and I was still awake; the Chinese takeaway we had had for dinner, an indulgence provided by Mrs. Devine, had made me extremely thirsty. There was no getting away from it, I needed a drink. On the way back from the kitchen, I could not resist listening at the door in the hall; it was very quiet, I thought, expecting five women in a confined area to create a reasonable volume of chatter. All of a sudden, the house fell eerily silent and I felt a strange wave of curiosity propelling me into the room, where the sight of the women sitting in a circle in the candlelit interior met my eyes; Mrs. King, dressed from head to toe in purple, sat in a prominent position with her head bowed.

What was going on?

CHAPTER 5 – A SURPRISE VISITOR

I sat down quietly to avoid disturbing the gathering and, as my eyes adjusted to the dimly lit room, I very soon became aware of another member of the group sitting in the shadows by the window – a little old woman, a black shawl covering her bony shoulders, knitting away at what I suspected was a cardigan or jumper.

Gradually, Mrs. King drew herself upright in her chair, dropping the hands of the women on either side of her.

"Well ladies, I hope you enjoyed the experience; my guide, as I said at the start, can be unpredictable."

"It was truly enlightening; we are so honoured at your presence in our little group," Mrs. Devine enthused, seeming to speak for them all.

It was at that point Mrs. King's eyes alighted on me.

"I see we have an intruder. Come here, my child."

"Katy, what are you doing?" screamed Mrs. Devine, leaping from her chair, "Go back up to bed at once!"

I had never heard Mrs. Devine speak to me in that tone before and, embarrassed, I turned to leave.

"No, wait – Mrs. Devine, please, I would love a chance to have a chat with this young woman."

I sidled up to Mrs King, who beckoned me to sit down next to her, which meant Laura Cain reluctantly had to move seats. "You must be wondering what we are doing here?" she asked.

"Well, I don't think it's a book club, that's for sure. Are you witches?" I blurted out.

Mrs. King chortled. "Witches? No, we're not witches, but I do understand why you would think that. No, I'm a medium, a spiritualist. You don't mind Katy knowing we're spiritualists, do you ladies?" She made a fleeting study of the room.

"Actually, I would rather that declaration didn't go any further, if you don't mind," emphasised Emily Stanton. "My husband is the vicar of this parish and I know full well he wouldn't approve; it might even mean a divorce."

"Yes, people around here wouldn't understand," added Laura Cain, "they're very narrow-minded."

"I should say they're narrow-minded," piped up Brenda Turley, "you should hear the comments I get when I go out. You would think nobody ever wore a mini skirt before."

Mrs. King coughed slightly, realising that the pelmet Brenda Turley called a skirt was showing more than an acceptable amount of leg.

"Yes of course, I see, well I'm sure Katy won't say anything, will you dear?"

I was very good at keeping my mouth shut and reassured everyone that their secret would not leave the room.

"Have you heard of spiritualism before, Katy?" Mrs. King continued.

"Oh yes, I have always been interested in the paranormal. When I was little …" I began, hesitating before I went on, worried these women would laugh at my declaration, "…when I was little I thought I had a spirit friend."

"Really, how fascinating. You say when you were little; you don't have one now?"

"Oh no, and – as I said – I only thought I had; I was going through a difficult time then, later I supposed I'd only imagined her."

Mrs King rose to her feet, stretching after sitting so long.

"First of all Katy, please call me Ursula – that goes for everyone here, 'Mrs. King' makes me feel ancient. In fact, to make us all feel at ease, I'm sure everyone here would like to be addressed by their first names, am I right?"

What could the other women say? Mrs. King, I mean Ursula, was certainly someone not to be argued with.

"Now, where should I begin? Let me try to explain. Children, we believe, especially ones who have experienced some kind of upset, are much more susceptible to the spirit world and perhaps your guardian angel, for I'm sure that's who she was, believes you don't need to feel her presence anymore – that's not to say she has left you, no, of course not."

I took a while to mull this idea through in my head. It made sense; every time I needed comfort when I was a small child, she seemed to be with me.

"I see, except when I was at my lowest, desperate for her presence, she wasn't there for me." Gabrielle's abrupt departure came flooding back into my thoughts. "You remember Mrs. Devine, I mean Flo, our au pair Gabrielle left suddenly. I loved her, Flo, I really loved her."

My unexpected outburst took them, and me, by surprise. Flo, not really happy about me calling her by her first name after all these years, put a very welcome arm around me.

"There, there, child, it was a long time ago, don't upset yourself. I think you're over-tired; it's way past your bedtime. How about I make you a nice warm drink, and see you back to bed?"

Flo was definitely a bit uncomfortable about me being there – after all, she had been left in charge of my welfare.

"You're right, Flo, I am tired. Thank you everyone, I hope I didn't spoil your evening, goodnight." I held out my hand to Ursula, taking hers in mine. "It was very nice to meet you. Sorry Ursula, where are my manners, is that your mother asleep in the corner? Please say goodnight to her for me. I hope she finishes that jumper she's been knitting."

Everyone looked towards the window where I could see the little old lady, whose head was now tilted to one side, fast asleep in mother's reading chair.

Laura let out a little cry. "What colour is the jumper?"

"What do you mean? You can see for yourself it's blue," I said, wondering if she needed her eyes tested.

"What is she wearing?" Laura's voice sounded desperate for an answer.

I did not understand. The little old lady was there for everyone to see, in fact, Laura's shrilled manner had now woken her and she was looking in my direction seemingly annoyed at having her sleep interrupted.

I sighed. "A black shawl over a grey dress."

I looked around at the rest of the women, expecting smiles at Laura's obvious inability to see what was right in front of her nose. Instead, they were all staring at me with expressions of disbelief.

"Katy, dear, can you ask her who she is?" Ursula insisted.

This was getting rather silly. "Ok. Hi, can you tell me your name?"

The old lady smiled and very articulately replied, "I'm Granny Cain, Katy, and Laura's my granddaughter."

"Sorry, I didn't recognise you. Yes, of course, Granny Cain, I remember you gave me fifty pence once to buy some sweets."

With that revelation Laura dropped to the floor – Flo ran to get her a glass of water, while the others fussed around her as they helped the unsteady woman to her feet.

The realisation I had just been in conversation with a dead person took me a bit of time to absorb. Apparently, Laura's grandmother had passed away two Christmas' before whilst knitting a jumper, a present for her daughter. It was Laura, who, desperate to make contact with her beloved grandmother, had dragged a reluctant Emily along to their first spiritualist meeting. From that beginning, the group had grown to the four women, who had all been drawn into the circle due to their own personal tragedies.

Whilst Laura recovered from her dizzy spell, I began to feel a little wobbly myself.

"Katy dear," Ursula began, "has anything like this ever happened to you before?"

Now to me this seemed rather a ridiculous question. How the hell would I have realised I had seen spirits that no one else could see; after all, Granny Cain, whose spirit had now evaporated from view, had looked and sounded real enough to me.

"Not that I'm aware of," I responded, trying to clarify my experiences once again. "I told you, I had felt a spirit presence years ago, and once when I was very young, I did think I saw a face of a woman at my bedroom window, but that's all."

"I see, well then I strongly believe you might have a very special gift, my dear, a gift that would be the envy of many who believe in the afterlife." Flo was now becoming slightly frantic about my well-being, and where all this talk of manifestations was leading.

"Ursula, I do think Katy is much too young and vulnerable to be encouraged into believing that she has some kind of 'gift' as you call it. I'm sure, in fact I'm positive, her mother would not approve and as she is my employer and has left Katy in my care, then I'm sorry but all this talk must cease," Flo emphasised, now very red in the face.

"Calm yourself, Flo. I agree she is too young, but you must admit that something quite wonderful happened here tonight, something all of us in this room were extremely fortunate to be privy to, would you not concur?"

A low murmur of agreement circumnavigated the room and before Flo could answer, Ursula continued, "Katy, how would you like to join us in our little meetings every so often – only if Flo agrees of course – just to sit, listen and learn, and even play a part if you feel the need. How would you feel about that?"

Well, what could I say? I was overcome with joy, to think that an adult of such importance believed I had something special to contribute.

Turning to Flo, I pleaded with her, "Please say yes, Flo, mother doesn't care what I do, she doesn't even have to know; it would be our secret. Please, please, Flo, say yes!"

Very reluctantly, Flo gave in to my pleas; consequently, over the next two years on the first Friday of every month I joined in with 'The Ladies Book Club' and learnt a lot about them and myself.

CHAPTER 6 – BECOMING A WOMAN

Mother never suspected anything untoward was happening in 'The Ladies Book Club' (the name we continued to use for our meetings, mainly for Emily's protection), because she was only too pleased to have a permanent babysitter for her Friday dalliances.

On those evenings, Ben always confined himself to his room, because the women downstairs terrified him. I, on the other hand, was becoming something of a celebrity in the small group, which now boasted two new members – spiritualist friends of Ursula's who only attended on the evenings I was due to be present.

The first was Molly Brightman, a rather austere city lawyer, who frankly put the wind up me a little. The second was Sue Kirk, a housewife; a much more approachable being, whose life seemed to revolve around her children. Unfortunately, those waiting excitedly on the possible reappearance of Granny Cain or any other spiritual manifestations were sorely disappointed. Months went by and I had nothing, not even a feeling of a spiritual presence, to contribute to the gathering. I soon realised I had no control on any visitations; that the spirit world would only use me when they saw fit.

***

It was due to her immense sadness that I confided in

Beth about my spiritual abilities one evening, when I bumped into her near the four willow trees which grew by the pond in the village. It was a very dark time in her life; apparently her father Max had been killed by a hit-and-run driver. My best friend had been so traumatised by the whole incident that I wanted to help soothe the incredible pain she was obviously going through, in the only way I knew how.

"You know they say that willow trees have a close spiritual connection. If we sit here quietly, perhaps something will happen."

I was not really sure what I expected; perhaps some sort of visitation from her dad, I think. However, sadly, there was no miraculous materialisation of any kind.

***

One particular Friday night when I was busy doing my maths homework in my room, a sudden frantic knock on my door stopped my train of thought.

"Katy, it's Laura, can you come downstairs? Flo is awfully upset; Ursula thought you might be able to help." Poor Flo, she was in a terrible state, sobbing all over Ursula who looked at me with some relief when I entered the dimly lit room.

"Katy, Flo's finally had a message from her son Brian and he mentioned you. Can you join us tonight please?"

I sat down next to Flo and held her hand. Brian, her only child, had died twenty years previous after contracting meningitis at the age of nine. I was not exactly sure what I was expected to do, so I simply followed Ursula's lead and closed my eyes. Sitting up straight in my chair, I tried to clear my mind. How long to sit in meditation before I admitted I was not feeling anything, I was unclear about; the minutes seemed to tick by in slow motion.

Eventually, I had to concede that – once again – nothing was going to happen. Gradually, I opened my eyes and was startled to perceive the previously darkened room now in a blaze of light and the women were nowhere to be seen. Walking towards me, from the apparent source of the illumination, his hands deep in his pockets, was a young boy in grey shorts, his cap awry on his mop of red curls.

"Is your name Brian?" I asked gently, not wanting to frighten him.

"Yes, miss. I hoped you would come; please tell my mum I love her and I'm always with her. Tell her not to be sad, I'm happy here, honest! Please tell her." With a grin, he turned and walked silently away.

The glow of light slowly faded, and gradually the women in the room came back into focus. After I had related Brian's message, Flo was the happiest I had seen her in years; it was as if she had been brought to life again. I felt truly blessed that I was able to bring such joy to someone I truly cared about.

***

Of course, 'The Ladies Book Club' was not the only thing happening in my life in my early teenage years. I was growing up fast. By the time I was fourteen and a half, I was at least three inches taller than mother and my body had developed; well, let us just say I was very pleased with my 34C.

One hot day in August, mother had to take Ben

into town to buy trainers and left me with strict instructions to clear the breakfast table and wash up before I took myself out into the garden to sunbathe. My chores completed, I grabbed my book, donned a very nice pair of sunglasses Flo had picked up for me in the market and settled down in the sun lounger on the large lawn attached to the patio. Slipping off my dress to reveal a skimpy little white bikini I only dared wear around the house, I thought I heard the click of the garden gate, but, looking up from my book, there seemed to be no sign of anyone so I decided I must have imagined it.

All of a sudden, from out of nowhere, Uncle Jack appeared on the grass next to me before I had time to grab my dress to cover my modesty.

"Well, well, what have we here? Katy is becoming a young woman at last." His leering eyes seemed to take in every part of my half-naked body, making me feel ashamed and dirty.

"Mother will be back soon," I stuttered, trying to cool my mother's lover, hoping he would go away. "Father's in the house, do you want to speak to him?"

"Nope, you're wrong, I saw him going out early this morning before I came over to … keep Rosemary company." His face drew closer to mine, while his rough fingers began to stroke my shoulder. "Such young, soft perfect skin," he remarked, his breathing now becoming more rapid.

I was terrified; more terrified than any interaction I had experienced from the spirit world. He picked up my bottle of sun cream and squirted a little onto his palms.

"Here, let Uncle Jack rub some cream onto those areas that are difficult to reach, don't want to burn this beautiful virgin skin."

My verbal protests were to no avail as he started searching my body. I prayed under my breath; prayed he would stop this invasion of my person, as his eager hand started the descent into my bikini bottoms.

"Katy, there you are! Oh, Mr. Palmer, did you want something?"

Relieved to see Flo striding into view from the side of the house, I jumped up, grabbing my dress. Immediately she had understood the situation and, with the anger of an enraged lioness, sent Uncle Jack off with a flea in his ear.

"I'm so relieved to see you Flo," I cried, falling into her arms. "I was so scared."

"There, there, Katy dear, you understand I must report him to your mother."

Of course, Flo was right: mother definitely needed to know about the sexual antics of her randy lover. Nevertheless, from that day on, whenever I was left alone, I made sure all the doors and windows were securely locked from unwanted intruders, however hot the weather.

Flo did tell mother, who naturally flew into a rage. However, her anger was not directed at Uncle Jack, no, it was directed at me! Yelling that I was a floozy and what did I expect when I dressed like a tramp? The next thing I knew, she had made an appointment for me with a new dentist from a town a few miles away, insisting he put in a National Health brace to straighten my teeth. The dentist tried to dissuade mother against the procedure, as my teeth were almost perfect, but when she offered him money, unethically he agreed to do it.

Overnight, I went from an emerging swan into

'Jaws'.

CHAPTER 7 – KNOW THINE ENEMY

I had been looking forward to going back to school in September, but now I kept my head down hoping no one would notice me. Of course, this was a vain hope and who should be one of the first people I should bump into? None other than Louise Turley, with her accompanying drooling gang of males and females.

"What have we here? Is it a bird? Is it a plane? No it's, let me see," she grabbed my hair, which mother insisted I now kept back in an unfashionably tight ponytail, before continuing her verbal abuse, "it's a freak, wow, who would want to snog that!"

The mixed group was now surrounding me, mocking my predicament.

"Now, now, move along, haven't you classes to go to?" Looking a little flustered, the headmaster emerged from his office, clearing the corridor with a wave of his hand.

***

How I cried into my pillow that night, dreading having to go back into school the following day.

"Are you ok?" Ben asked, putting his head around my bedroom door. "If anyone is giving you grief over your braces, just let me know, I've been practicing my judo."

Darling Ben, he so wanted to play the big brother and protect me. Fortunately, over the next few months, the bullying eased a bit as everyone got used to seeing the 'freak' – as the entire school now knew me.

***

One of the busiest times of year at Hill Farm was when families from Willow Green and the surrounding villages descended on us to collect our much-coveted Christmas trees. This was an exciting time for Ben and me, as we were able to help father sort and sell the trees for a small remuneration. With the proceeds, we were able to buy Christmas presents for our entire family and, more often than not, there was a little over to treat ourselves.

Meanwhile, at school, it was the end of term carol concerts, school plays and the dreaded exams. Following a particularly stressful English Literature paper, I popped into the loo, from where the sound of someone crying in one of the cubicles made me stop and listen.

"Are you ok, do you need help?" I enquired to the unknown pupil beyond the locked door.

"Get lost, freak, I don't need yours or anyone else's help." I recognised the voice of Louise Turley straight away. She did not have to say anymore; I did what I had come in for and left.

***

My grandparents and Penny were always a joyful part of our Christmas ritual, but being cooped up for such long periods all together, well, I just had to get out sometimes – so I offered to walk the little dog most days. It was a mile or so into the village and back, but I enjoyed the freedom and usually took a short cut along the bridleways of a neighbouring farm, as this was as much as the little mite could manage.

One frosty morning, when the whole countryside looked as if the White Witch from Narnia had cast her spell, I caught sight of two figures standing some way away, by an old rust-bucket of a car, apparently in the middle of a heated argument.

Drawing closer, I realised it was Louise Turley and a boy from the upper sixth. I could not hear exactly what they were saying, but Louise seemed very distressed. He was trying to get back in the car while Louise was pulling at his coat, screaming loudly. Without warning, he turned, raised his arm, and struck her hard about her face, knocking her down onto the frozen earth. Glaring hatefully at the girl now sprawled upon the hard ground, he climbed triumphantly back into his vehicle. The wheels of his car spun several times on the icy verge, before disappearing with a roar down the narrow, winding country lane.

Forgetting for the moment that it was my enemy lying there in an undignified heap, I ran to her aid. With blood streaming from her nose, I tried to hand her a tissue, but she simply brushed my hand away, yelling, "Get away bitch, who asked for your help!"

I had had as much as I could take; here we were, miles from anyone, and she still could not bear me around her.

"Louise, enough is enough, forget for once you hate me, take my arm and try to stand. Don't look at me like that," I warned, seeing the scowl on her face, "accept the fact you need my help; you could die out here of hyperthermia." Taken aback by my uncharacteristic dominant manner, she finally accepted my arm as I helped her struggle to her feet. "Does it hurt anywhere? Can you walk?"

"What do you care? Just leave me to die!"

"Your mum wouldn't forgive me if I did."

"My mum? You don't know my mum, and anyway she wouldn't care what happened to me."

I wanted to tell Louise I had grown to know her mum, Brenda, very well over the past few years. Knew of her torment following the loss of her twin sister Beryl at an early age, when a game of tag they were playing had gone tragically wrong. How she had watched helplessly as Beryl had slipped and fallen into the path of a speeding car, which had thrown her high into the air before her broken body had come to rest on the tarmac road beside the distraught Brenda. I wanted to tell Louise I had spoken to Beryl, bringing peace to her mother's suffering. I wanted to tell her but, of course, I couldn't; she wouldn't believe me anyway.

Very slowly, with Louise wincing in discomfort with every step she took, we eventually made it to the village. Finally reaching her house, cautiously I rang the doorbell. With a flourish, the face of Brenda appeared on the other side of the door, ecstatic to set her obviously-intoxicated eyes on me and, almost forgetting herself for a moment, she bellowed, "Katy..." until she noticed her battered daughter leaning against the wall. "Louise, what the hell happened to you?"

I helped Brenda manoeuvre Louise into the hallway before making my excuses to leave.

"I'll let Louise explain what happened, Brenda," I

said quietly. "As I'm here, I think I'll pop next door and call on Flo." Brenda nodded and smiled gratefully, before guiding her daughter away to the comfort of their sitting room.

It was a funny thing, but after all this time I had never been to Flo's house. Of course there had never been reasons why I should have done; as far as mother was concerned, she was the hired help and – apart from Uncle Jack – she believed one should not mix socially with employees. Anyway, here I was in front of No.14 Parkside Road, Flo's semi-detached council dwelling, and, as I pushed at the creaking wooden gate and walked up the concrete path, my anticipation rose as to the reception I would receive. I waited several minutes before the glass-panelled door opened and Flo appeared, obviously stunned to see me standing on her doorstep. Immediately, she threw her arms around me and ushered me into the warmth of her front room, where a much-appreciated fire was roaring away.

"Katy, dear, you look absolutely frozen, come and sit by the fire. Can I get you a warm drink and perhaps a nice bowl of water for Penny?"

"Yes, thanks Flo, I hope I'm not calling at a bad time, only ... I was in the area, so I thought it would be rude not to visit."

I was certainly relieved to be regaining the feeling in my fingers and toes again, and, as Penny curled up in a prime position in front of the fire, her nose and her front paws almost being singed by the burning embers, I began to survey my surroundings.

The ambience of the entire room was quite a surprise, as it seemed to be stuck in a time warp. Not that I was up to date with interior design – not at all –

but I did have an idea about the 1970's from old films I'd watched after dinner on Sunday afternoons. The bright swirls in shades of oranges and browns on the carpet, I felt, seriously clashed with the patterned multi-coloured wallpaper. A black leather suite, which had obviously seen better days, had been thrust against the walls of the small room, seemingly trying to give it a feeling of space.

Eventually, my eyes alighted on what I realised was the reason Flo had not wanted to change the décor: photos upon photos, in a variety of frames, of a once-happy family – Flo, her husband, and Brian. I felt myself smiling back at the cheeky young boy, with red tousled hair, whose grin seemed to be focused in my direction.

"Of course, you'll recognise my Brian," Flo commented, as she re-entered the room with a tray of drinks and turkey sandwiches, making me jump with embarrassment at my intrusion into her life. "The picture you have in your hand was taken on his first day at school, he was really excited and had practised tying his tie for days beforehand." She beamed with pride as she set the tray down on the coffee table, before handing me a mug of steaming hot chocolate, which I took eagerly from her grasp. We sat chatting together for a while as I slowly demolished the meaty sandwiches so perfectly cut into triangles.

"Have you lived in this house all your married life, Flo?" I enquired, genuinely interested.

"Yes, just about. When Harold and I first married, we lived with his mother – oh my god what a disaster that was, the interfering old so-and-so. I was never good enough for her precious son and did she let me know it, every single day she was alive. We had put our names down on the council waiting list the day after our wedding day, and when we found Brian was on the way, we finally got this place – our little palace we called it. We were happy here for a long time." Flo picked up a picture of Brian "Well, you know the rest. After he left us, I felt I had also lost my husband, my best friend; we never talk about him now."

I moved from the comfort of the chair next to the fire and joined Flo on the settee, taking her hand in mine. Dear, kind Flo, who had always been there for me and Ben, I could not bear to think she was so unhappy and lonely; no wonder she was content to spend so much time at the farm looking after us.

"You've got me and Ben, Flo, and don't forget the 'Ladies Book Club'; they're all your friends too." I beamed, trying to bring a smile to her face.

"Of course, you're right Katy, I'm just feeling sorry for myself that's all, it's the time of the year, Christmas, you know can be so lonely. Anyway," suddenly perking up, she leapt to her feet, "I must get you home, Harold should be back with the van any minute, I'll run you up to the farm as soon as he gets here. I'll just give your mother a quick ring first, if you need the loo it's the door on the right at the top of the stairs."

I reached the first floor before I realised it had not registered with me whether Flo said left or right, but as she was now deep in conversation on the phone in the hall, I decided to try the first door I came to, which happened to be on the left. Carefully, I pushed down the handle and entered, but it was immediately apparent I had made a mistake.

I had observed the lounge was from a time gone by, but here in front of me was the bedroom of a much-loved son, which morbidly did not seem to have been touched since his death – apart from a bit of dusting. It was a museum of artefacts; toys and books were scattered everywhere. The blue-painted walls were covered with football posters of his favourite team, Chelsea. I suddenly felt an enormous sadness descend upon me, a sadness that curiously drew me towards the window. Peering from the dizzy heights of the upstairs room, I realised that from this elevated position I could see straight into Brenda's garden next door. Both gardens backed on to a small wooded area. As I strained to see, a brick-built structure caught my eye.

"It's a well." Flo's sudden appearance startled me. "It was here long before these houses were built and apparently it was once the main source of water for this part of the village."

"I'm so sorry, Flo," I stuttered, once again mortified at being caught in a situation which could be perceived as being nosey. "I was looking for the bathroom."

"Katy, you know you're the first person to step into this room, apart from me and Harold, since … I know Brian would be thrilled you're here, I know I am." We hugged and cried until we heard Harold coming through the front door.

Ten minutes later, Flo's van drew up in front of Hill Farm. I reached over and kissed the cheek of the woman who had been more of a mother to me than my own, promising I would visit her at her house again very soon.

CHAPTER 8 – AN UNSOLICITED ENCOUNTER

With the New Year celebrations behind us, I was more than pleasantly surprised that at last Louise was keeping her distance from me; on the unavoidable occasions when our paths did cross, I was sure – no, I was positive – to my amazement, she even managed a sort of smile in my direction.

The other good news was that my braces completely fell apart one morning during breakfast, and father, unaware of mother's aspiration to make me as undesirable to the opposite sex as she possibly could, especially Uncle Jack, made an emergency appointment with our family dentist who removed the vile contraption from my very-relieved mouth. So now, several months on, with my thick wavy black hair flowing freely and pink lip-gloss applied carefully on my full lips, at last I felt confident enough to join the youth club at the village hall in Willow Green. I had heard so much about the goings on at this social centre from my friends at school that I could not wait to enrol and meet, let's face it, the fantasy of most girls of my age – boys.

The village hall was the pulsating hub of everything that went on in the area, from the 'Mother and Baby' group to the WI. I was really not sure what to expect, as I nervously alighted from father's Land Rover. Several small gatherings of teenagers had already collected in the car park; most had been religiously dropped off, no doubt like me, by their anxious parents, who had prayed silently that whoever was running the club could be completely trusted to be in charge of the welfare of their treasured son or daughter. I am positive my father felt the same way, but held back about his uncertainties. All he mumbled was, "Have a good time, I'll pick you up at ten."

I greeted my new friends, Abby and Chrissie, enthusiastically and, giggling excitedly, we merged with the rest of the gathering, eager to enter this den of social interaction. Loud rap music hit us as we crossed the threshold, putting us all immediately in the party mood. Several small rooms ran off from the main hall, where games of pool and table tennis were already taking place – I thought it was all wonderful.

Then I caught sight of him: a tall blond god with strong broad shoulders and piercing green eyes, standing nonchalantly with a group of male friends who were hovering over the CD player, while at the same time eyeing up the girls as they strutted past.

"That's Joshua, he only moved here a couple of months ago," drooled Abbey, appearing at my side, "surprised you haven't noticed him at school; most of the girls in our year have – gorgeous, isn't he?" He certainly was, although, I believed, in reality way out of my league.

Those three hours of pleasurable, flirtatious fun passed very quickly. I looked at my watch: it was nearly ten and father would be arriving soon, the last thing I wanted was for him to come into the hall; how humiliating would that be? Therefore, I said my goodbyes and went outside to wait for him.

It was a cool, crisp clear night and the full moon was already high in the sky. Suddenly, from the shadows behind me, I heard a match strike and the smell of a cigarette wafted in my direction.

"Haven't seen you here before, you're quite a babe." I spun round and found I was confronting the very low-life from the sixth form I had seen with Louise Turley, who I had since found out was called Stephen Hamilton. As he drew closer, toxic fumes of tobacco and booze filled my now-irritated nostrils.

"Do you mind?" I exclaimed haughtily, determined that this piece of scum was not going to intimidate me.

"I don't if you don't. How about a quickie behind the bus shelter?" he growled, grabbing me unexpectedly around the waist, pulling me eagerly towards him. I could feel his throbbing member beneath his trousers. Disgust overflowed me as he tried to rub himself up against my leg.

"Get lost!" I shrieked, trying to push him away with all the strength I could muster – terrifyingly, he was far too strong. While trying to drag my rigid body back into the shadows, his slimy tongue entered my mouth preventing me from uttering any further cries.

"What the fuck! Get off her, you rich bastard!" yelled my saviour. Managing to wrench my attacker off me, Joshua drew back his arm and threw a swift punch to my assailant's jaw, causing him to fall heavily to the ground. Instantly, scores of people enveloped us, jeering at the individual now sprawled unceremoniously on the tarmac of the car park.

"Are you ok, Katy? I've called the police, they should be here any minute," cried Abby, as she put a most welcome arm around me. I looked around for Joshua, eager to thank my gallant hero. However his mates, who were apparently congratulating him on the punch of the century, now surrounded him, making it impossible for me to get his attention.

The pulsating blue light of the local police car, which materialized at the same time as father's Land Rover, put a stop to any further activity. Sprinting to my side, the image in front of father took some explaining. In fact, the police had to hold him back as he was ready to land one on my attacker himself. Unfortunately, as he eventually led me away to the safety of his vehicle, I knew that my dalliance into the local youth club scene would definitely not be repeated – however hard I pleaded.

***

Naturally, the incident was the talk of the village for weeks and, of course, my friends in 'The Ladies Book Club' were full of anxiety for my welfare.

"I'm not totally surprised at his behaviour, I'm sorry to say," exclaimed Laura one Friday as she bit hard into a rather stale digestive biscuit, which had been occupying the space at the bottom of the biscuit barrel.

"Spoilt rotten by his parents from the day he was born; the stories I could tell you about his behaviour when he came into the post office – out of control, always out of control!"

"Of course, he is an only child. Not that I'm making that an excuse for him, but Barbara Hamilton gave me the impression he has frequently been unfairly blamed for various indiscretions," Emily emphasised. "I remember when money went missing after one of our WI jumble sales, several members were sure he had stolen it, but when – weeks later –

the bag and the money was discovered at the back of the cleaning cupboard, well, Barbara gave us all a look of smug satisfaction."

"I wonder why he was expelled from his private school." Flo pondered. "If he hadn't been, he probably wouldn't have been at the youth club that night and Katy wouldn't have gone through that horrible ordeal," she remarked, turning to me with a sympathetic smile.

"Well, he was and, quite frankly, I don't want to talk about it anymore and anyway I hear he's off to university soon so, good riddance! Now, can we get on with the meeting please?"

The aftermath of the incident with Stephen Hamilton, the high-and-mighty son of my former headmaster, had propelled me into unwelcomed celebrity status at school and, frankly, I wanted to get away from this notoriety when I was among my friends. It was not that I was ungrateful for all the concern, on the contrary, but I hankered to put the visions of that night behind me.

Currently, our Ladies Book Club meetings were being held in the small, but perfect, one-bedroomed flat above the post office, where Laura had lived ever since becoming the Post Mistress. It had a very feminine, homely environment about it, making us all feel very comfortable. Sadly, Ursula had been absent due to illness for several months now and consequently it had been decided not to hold our meetings as frequently until she was well again, given she was the lynch-pin holding us all together.

While Laura lit the candles scattered around the room, we sat together, finally in silence, holding hands, trying to channel our thoughts from the troubles of this world to the higher plane of the spirit world. It had been a long time since I had had any contact with the supernatural so, to be frank, I was not expecting anything to happen this evening and anyway, my mind wasn't feeling very spiritual; I was thinking of my geography assignment which was now well overdue.

All of a sudden my head dropped forward, followed by a searing pain in my back and shoulders, which forced out a pitiful cry through my lips, startling those around me. I was quiet for several minutes afterwards until I emerged from my transient state.

"Can I have a glass of water?" I asked, briefly gasping for air. Brenda jumped to her feet and scurried to the kitchen, re-emerging moments later clutching a large glass of ice-cold water straight from the tap, while the rest of the group looked on nervously at my apparent distress.

Eventually regaining control, I turned to Emily, taking her hand in mine as tears welled in her eyes. She had originally joined the group due to the tragic death of her beloved father, Alfred Reed, who had lost control of his bike one evening whilst cycling home from the pub. The unfortunate man had ended up in a ditch, where he had laid for several hours on one of the coldest nights of that particular year. Her husband, Reverend Stanton, had made the gruesome discovery of his stiff, frozen body while walking the family dog. The rumour that spread around the village, following his premature death, was that he was drunk and should not have tried to ride home. Emily had always felt cheated she had not had the chance to say goodbye to the man who had been both father and mother to her, as her mother had died shortly after she was born. Gently, I related her father's message.

"Your father says he loves you and not to be sad; he's happy because he's with your mum again." Following those words, she sobbed uncontrollably for several minutes.

"Thank you Katy, I'll never forget this, never."

Eventually, after several cups of tea, the evening ended and the women went their weary ways, but as I prepared to leave, Laura gently touched my arm. "Can we have a chat before you go?" she asked quietly, closing the door. I was intrigued. "I wondered, Katy, if you fancied a Saturday job working in the post office?"

"Oh, thanks Laura, yes that would be great, I'm sure nobody at home will object. Actually I wanted a word too, about exactly what happened tonight." I began, somewhat hesitantly, unsure if Laura was the right person to share the knowledge I had gained from Emily's father. "Alfred told me something I wasn't sure whether I should relate to Emily," I looked down at the floor, searching for the right words, "he said ... he wasn't drunk and it wasn't an accident, the night he died, in fact the wheel had mysteriously come adrift from his bike – he strongly believed someone had tampered with it."

Laura looked perplexed. "Oh my god, I understand why you didn't tell Emily. If you are seeking my advice, Katy, then forget what he told you; it was such a long time ago. If you pass this information on to her, that there was a possibility Alfred was, dare I say it, murdered, then it could destroy her."

She was right, of course; and, as an afterthought, it would probably not be of any interest to the police – as if they would believe a story from a sixteen-year-old girl who claimed to have had a conversation with a deceased being! They would laugh in my face – perhaps even lock me away in a mental institution and throw away the key. No, I would try to put the whole incident to the back of my mind.

Peddling fast towards home on that warm, sultry summer evening, with the sun lying low in the vivid red sky before me, I thought of Alfred passing along the very track on which my wheels were now trundling, praying that he had not suffered; that death had taken him instantly.

CHAPTER 9 – JOSHUA AND ME

"Can't believe you're eighteen already Kate, the years, where did they go?"

It was midweek and I was at Doctor Daniels' surgery receiving a tetanus shot following an accident on the farm, where a splinter of wood had unwontedly implanted itself in the ball of my foot. I looked at him closely, this aging man before me, curious to know how old he was. I calculated he must be at least seventy by now; surely, I contemplated, way past retirement age. I thought of all the hundreds, no thousands, of people who had passed through his surgery; so many ailments, so many stories, and so many secrets, after all, it was a doctor's duty not to tell.

"So, have you finished school now, young lady?" he enquired. I nodded. I had never been any good with needles and the size of the one in front of me about to penetrate my arm certainly looked bigger than usual. I winced, with my eyes tightly closed, trying hard not to cry. "There, all done, shouldn't be any need for another one for at least ten years, you can roll your sleeve down now," he instructed.

"Thank you, Doctor Daniels. By the way, you won't be seeing me around the village for a while, I'm off to university in September," I piped up; relieved the ordeal was now behind me.

"Wonderful. What are you studying?"

"English and psychology in London," I announced

proudly. I was the first of my family to go to university, so for once in our family unit I had been made to feel special.

"And your mother, is she keeping well? I haven't seen her at any village functions for a while."

No, I thought, you would not have. Mother was becoming a stranger not only in the village but in our house as well. She had insisted, the previous year, that father purchase a small holiday bungalow off the Dorset coast, so they had somewhere to escape to. Fortunately for us, it was mother who was doing all the escaping, leaving us to lead a much more harmonious life. Even father was around more, and the other day I actually listened to him singing in the bathroom, a joyous sound I had never heard before. The subject of 'divorce' had not yet reared its ugly head into their conversations, as far as I was aware, and as for Uncle Jack, well he left soon after the Dorset property was purchased – enough said.

"Mother's fine, busy with our holiday home in Dorset ... lots of improvements to make, I understand," I lied, hobbling to the door before turning and smiling at the all-knowing doctor, who smiled back at me and nodded.

Ben was dutifully lingering in the crowded waiting-room, ready to run me home. Ever since passing his driving test the day after his seventeenth birthday, he had the pleasure of driving father's Land Rover, and these days he never seemed to walk anywhere. Glancing around the room, I could not help but notice the bent head of a tousled-haired young man: my dreamboat, Joshua Bannerman. I blushed profusely as he looked up from the magazine he was reading.

"Hi Josh, you playing next Sunday?" Ben asked, while I cringed with embarrassment.

"Wouldn't miss it, it will be the last game before I leave for uni. Are you coming to the match, Kate?" he posed, looking me straight in the eyes.

"You never go, do you, Kate? Hates cricket, she does, finds it boring. Anyway, see you on Sunday then." With the humiliation over, Ben helped me to father's vehicle and, as soon as the door was securely shut, I spoke my mind.

"How dare you speak for me. He asked me! He asked me!" I shouted, realising that my own brother had just ripped away the opportunity I had been dreaming about for months – the opportunity to have a conversation with Joshua.

"What are you getting your knickers in a twist for?" he exclaimed, turning and looking at me. "You don't fancy him, do you?" The look on my face said it all. "You do, you fancy Josh, oh my god. Well come then, come on Sunday, you can help the WI with the sandwiches."

***

Sunday, the day of the match, dawned. Father and Ben were all togged-up as usual in their whites, ready to do battle on the village green against the folk of the neighbouring village of Torrington. There had been a strong rivalry between the two villages for years; fortunately it was always good-humoured but, even so, each side did their very best to win. Apparently, Joshua was our star player, so was put into bat first. While ball after ball was smashed across the green, I was kept busy with Flo and the women from the WI, buttering bread and making copious cups of tea.

"I was surprised to see you here, Kate," Flo commented. "It's a nice surprise though." She glanced out from the pavilion just as loud clapping broke out around the grounds, a reaction to the fact that Joshua had just knocked up a hundred runs. "Are you here because of that young man out there, my dear?"

"Of course she is," Emily interjected, "quite understandable, if you ask me; he's a real dish. Excuse me, George is about to bat, promised I'd watch him." Quickly, she darted outside and down the steps of the pavilion to support the Reverend as he took up his place by the crease. I looked over towards the wickets where Joshua was waiting anxiously for the next ball to be bowled. Was it so obvious to my friends – my infatuation?

"Don't wait too long, Kate, he won't be around forever," Flo pointed out.

"I know, but … it's no good, I clam up whenever he's around."

"I find that hard to believe, after all the riveting conversations we've had over the years. Try and forget he's a male of the species, you're a beautiful and intelligent young woman – if anything, I bet he's in awe of you." Dear Flo, once again she knew the right thing to say.

Barbara Hamilton's sudden call for tea over the loudspeaker system brought the match to a temporary halt. I grinned at Flo. "Ok, it's now or never."

With my confidence raised, I began to carry a large plate of perfectly-cut ham sandwiches out onto the porch and … damn, I tripped in front of everyone and watched in slow motion as the delicately arranged fare left the plate and rose high in the air, before falling to earth among a colourful bed of geraniums. I thought I would die of embarrassment.

Running to my aid yet again, Joshua helped me gather the demolished food from the flowerbed.

"I don't think they can be saved," he declared, stating the obvious.

Staring at the crumbled mess and then at each other, we started to laugh. Oh, how we laughed. With our tea and a fresh batch of sandwiches, we sat together under an old oak tree, enjoying each other's company until the game resumed. I was in a dream. When the match finally ended, with Willow Green having a resounding win by sixty-three runs, Joshua and I said our goodbyes but not before we made a date for the cinema the following evening.

***

The place was packed, but as I watched the muscles of Arnold Schwarzenegger flex in *Terminator 3*, I felt Joshua's arm glide over my uncovered shoulders, I squealed within with the pleasure his touch was bringing me as he gently stroked my skin. Slowly, he bent forward and I tasted his lips for the first time; a long, lingering kiss that simply took my breath away. With my pleasure from his touch intensifying, his left hand began its move beneath my strappy top, searching for my breast beneath, and when his fingers eventually found its destination I let out a quiet moan. The end of the film came all too soon. Walking hand in hand towards the bus stop, we turned to face each other, once again our lips meeting and our passions heightening.

Unexpectedly pulling away from me, he announced, "You don't know how long I've wanted to kiss you, to hold you, to touch you." I could not believe what I was hearing; it seemed he had had the same feelings that I had been harbouring all these years. I admitted to him that I felt the same. He continued his declaration, "I don't want to push you into anything you're uncomfortable with … I mean, we should take things slowly we're both off to uni soon … I don't want us to make promises we might find hard to keep."

I understood very clearly what he was saying: he had just invaded my body with a quick grope but he did not want to make any commitments to me, after all, with three years of university in front of us, he wanted to be free to meet and, let us be honest, shag anyone he wanted to. At least, I believed that is what he was trying to tell me. The rest of the walk to the bus stop was a little subdued. As we said our goodnights he tried to change the mood by asking me out for a drink the following evening. I couldn't say no, could I?

I made up my mind that if we only had a short time together, then so be it. Two glorious weeks of socialising and long country walks followed, before we had to say our farewells, promising to text or phone each other when time allowed.

Driving through the crowded London streets in father's Land Rover, packed full of my possessions, I should have felt excited. Here I was, a girl from the country, embarking on a fresh chapter in my life, new people and new experiences – however, all I could think of was Joshua and how much I loved him.

CHAPTER 10 – YOUNG LOVERS

I decided I was not going to be the first one to text – I didn't want to look too desperate. However, as the weeks flew by and still I had not heard from him, so many 'what ifs' were milling through my head. What if he's already found someone else? What if he's forgotten me? Not hearing from him was driving me crazy. Eventually, with some difficulty, I tried to push these thoughts from my head and I finally began to concentrate on my studies. Then, towards the end of October, I received the first of several plain postcards from Joshua – much more romantic, I thought, than a text.

Hi Kate,
Sorry about the postcard, only lost my phone on the bus. Digs fine, room of my own but shared kitchen and bathroom. Course seems ok, Sheffield nice area. Fresher's week was parties all the way; now time to get down to studying. Yuk.
Josh

I reciprocated, also on a plain postcard.

Hi Josh,
Glad you are settling in. Sorry about your phone, I know I'd be lost without mine. London is full on, like you parties most nights, so no time yet to miss home. Flatmates taking a bit of getting use to though, but I'm sure eventually I'll be fine.
Kate

Hi Kate,
Me again. Still no phone, saving up. Looking forward to Christmas, although I'll have loads of work to bring home. Found some bar work to help pay the bills – which is a relief. Never worked so hard! Hope you're ok. See you soon. Josh

Next time I wrote, I made the decision to splash out and purchased a rather colourful picture of the changing of the Guards, outside Buckingham Palace.

Dear Josh,
I hope you enjoyed Christmas as much as I did. Thanks again for the necklace; you shouldn't spend your money on me. It was a great New Year's Eve party, what I can remember, hope I didn't embarrass myself. I did feel a bit ill the next day. Anyway, it's back to work. Kate.
PS Hope you like the card, I know you have a phone now, but somehow, writing is so much more personal, don't you think?

Dear Kate,
Been up all night studying economic theory, thought I would just drop you a quick line, I've never drunk so much coffee before. In my tired state thought I saw you today, but when she turned round, well, she definitely wasn't you. I'm beginning to wonder if I'm cut out for uni, if I don't pass the final exams ... god, I'm rambling, more tired than I thought, even the coffee's not working now. Best wishes, Josh.
PS loved the card, this one is of uni building where I have my lectures. Agree that cards are more personal and you can keep them forever.

A TROUBLED SOUL

Dear Josh,
Sorry you're beginning to doubt whether uni is for you, apparently it's not unusual at this stage in the first year to start to have qualms about one's abilities, I'm sure you'll be fine, just try and keep positive. Ben sends his regards and hopes you'll be up for playing cricket when you get home. Very best wishes, Kate x
PS visited Madame Tussauds last week, that's where I bought this card. By the way, forever is a very long time.

Dear Kate,
Aren't we sounding like a psychologist already! You are right though, just taken my last exam, feel quite confident now. Any plans for the summer hols? Dad's got me a job working with him in his law firm, must say, not looking forward to it. Will we get a chance to meet up sometime? If you want to, that is? Tell Ben I have managed a couple of matches for uni so keeping my hand in. Yours, Josh x
PS Sorry my card's a bit boring, Sheffield Town Hall, not quite as interesting as wax works. Was that Beckham in the background by the way? I hope we do have time Kate.

Dear Josh,
I'll have a job too over the summer, in the village post office, Miss Cain has broken her wrist running in a half marathon (don't ask) so has asked me to work full time. Yes, I'd love to meet up, will phone you when I get home. Very best wishes, Kate x
PS Beckham and Posh. I hope we do too, have time I mean.

The slower pace of village life after London took me a while to get used to; also, I arrived home with even more stuff than I had left with, together with an enormous bin bag of dirty washing. Flo took one look at it and sighed.

"I did try and keep up with it all, honestly Flo, but with exams and getting out of my digs, well, the washing just got away from me." I owned up. "Don't worry, I don't expect you to do it for me, I'm quite independent now." I beamed sincerely.

"Kate dear, you've earned a holiday, it won't take me long to get through this lot. By the way, Laura was asking when you'd be arriving; I told her you'd give her a ring as soon as you got back."

***

"Well, what's the gossip Laura?" I asked sometime later as we sat together in her flat.

"There's so much, where to start? Of course, the group has not been meeting as often since you've been away. Ursula is still very poorly unfortunately; women's troubles I think. Brenda is excited though: Louise has just been signed up with a high profile modelling agency in London."

"I know. I'd heard she'd been spotted while she was working behind the counter in Woolworths. I really hope all goes well for her." Laura gave me a doubtful look. "Truthfully, we had our differences years ago, but we got through that; we weren't exactly friends at the end, but we certainly weren't enemies anymore."

"Oh yes, and Stephen Hamilton was home for a while, but now apparently he's moved to London. Barbara was boasting the other day that he has a good job in the Bank of England; no doubt he will be running it soon, I expect." Laura gave a chuckle before continuing, "Running it, not ruining it, I hope, for all our sakes. How are things with you, did you enjoy your first year?"

"Yes, it was great. Expensive to live there though so father and I have decided it's best I live at home for the next two years and commute into London for lectures. I'll miss the social side I guess, but it will help keep the costs down."

Laura looked thoughtful. "How do you feel about living here?"

"What, with you? There's only one bedroom, isn't there? I know we're friends Laura, but …"

"Oh no Kate," she chortled, "I've been thinking for a while about moving into my grandmother's cottage at the end of the village. If you remember, I was left it in her will and I've been renting it out. The current tenants have just given me notice, so now would be a good time to take possession of it myself."

"That sounds ideal, but rent … I couldn't afford much I'm afraid, perhaps you'd be better off asking someone who could pay what it's worth."

"Well, as long as you're working in the shop, let's call it a perk."

Consequently, that is how I made the transition into independence and finally left home. Of course, it didn't happen overnight; I had the long summer months first to enjoy in the bosom of my family, and in the strong arms of Josh.

***

"How many acres is it?" he inquired one evening when we were taking a late stroll along the lanes, past the orchards full of ripening fruit.

"Thousands," I replied mockingly, "absolutely thousands. Come this way, I want to show you my secret place." Guiding him by his hand, I led Josh down a rather overgrown track that led to a weather-worn stile. "I used to come here a lot when I was a small child, with our au pair Gabrielle." I looked nostalgically out into the overgrown meadow that father had decided to give back to nature. "Come on, let's go in."

I soon began to regret wearing shorts as the high grasses wiped their seed-filled heads on my bare skin. Reaching the far end of the field, we stopped and Josh removed his sweatshirt before placing it purposefully on the hard, dry ground. We lay with our arms folded behind our heads, looking up into the beautiful blue sky, watching as the numerous cloud formations drifted along in the evening breeze. Unaware of our presence below, flocks of birds flew overhead calling loudly to each other as they gathered their last morsels of the day.

I rolled over and kissed him; kissed him hard with all the passion I could muster. I wanted him to know I loved him and that after all this time, there was still no one else. He pushed me gently back onto his sweatshirt; his tanned, handsome features were now in front of me, instead of the white fluffy clouds. Slowly, he unbuttoned my blouse and began to fondle my breasts. I was thankful I had put on my new lacy bra, which he skilfully removed.

"You're so beautiful, Kate," he soothed, eyeing every part of my half-naked body, "but please say if you want me to stop, as I said before I don't want to force you into anything you'll regret later, I care too much about you."

I kissed him passionately again to reassure him. "Josh, believe me ... I don't want you to stop." I slipped off my shorts, exposing my skin-coloured thong, whilst he removed his clothes with intensifying enthusiasm.

"Wait," he cried, unexpectedly turning away from me. Removing a condom from his pocket, he slid it over his erect manhood before turning back to me – ultimately our young willing bodies came together. He tried to be gentle as he entered me. I had dreamt about this moment for such a long time, but I certainly had not anticipated the pain now shooting up inside me. When Josh had completed the act, he lay beside me, exhausted. So, I contemplated, that was sex ... We cuddled and kissed for a while before dressing.

"Are you alright?" he asked, obviously concerned at my quiet demeanour.

"I'm fine ... we'd better get back before father comes out to find us." He spun me around to face him.

"Kate, it was your first time; if you give me another chance it will get better, I promise."

Later that night as I gazed at the reflection of my face in the mirror, I wondered if to the outside world I looked any different? I certainly felt different.

***

My next trip to Doctor Daniels surgery was, to be frank, most mortifying. I had known the good doctor all my life and here I was admitting I was planning to have sex before marriage, and could he prescribe the birth control pill? Of course, his probable judgement was that I was being responsible; after all, I was more than nineteen, so well over the age of consent.

The rest of the summer flew by in a whirl and yes, Josh was right, the sex definitely got better. In truth, whenever we had the opportunity we made love; it was simply wonderful. Then, about the same time as Josh left for Sheffield, I got the keys for Laura's flat – which was henceforth known as Kate's flat.

I had so many visitors in the first few weeks that I did not have time to feel lonely. Flo turned up almost every day with some excuse or another and Ben frequently called in because the flat was on the way to his favourite pub. We also started to hold our meetings on a monthly basis again, with the exception of Ursula (who was still poorly) and her two friends, neither of whom we had seen for a long time. This was a secret part of my life; I had not yet confided in Josh – simply because I was not sure he would understand. How we had managed all these years to keep our gatherings from our respective families, I do not know. As far I was aware no one, apart from my friend Beth, knew of our beliefs in the afterlife; they just thought we all enjoyed reading.

The nights were the worst, as I strove to grow accustomed to the new sounds from the cobbled street outside. Of course, the traffic in London hardly ever stopped its constant drone but here, in the middle of the village, it was usually peaceful like the farm. Until, that is, a late night drinker staggered down the path, kicking over empty milk bottles left out on doorsteps, or the sudden sound of feuding tomcats fighting over territory, abruptly interrupted my slumber.

On one of these occasions, when I had finally

managed to drift back to sleep again, I experienced a disturbing dream. I was sitting on a bench by the willow tree, people-watching – I should say dead-people-watching. For every being that passed by I knew was no longer of this world. How long I sat there I was unsure, before I saw her walking purposely towards me; I recognised her at once, even after all these years, the woman I had seen from the window who had appeared to me on my fourth birthday. She smiled affectionately as she held out her arms in greeting, I rose and began drifting towards her until we were almost touching, then serenely she disappeared into an encroaching mist, just as I was awoken by the tuneful sound of my mobile phone.

"Morning sleepy-head. Just wanted to hear your voice." Josh, oh how I longed for him. This term we had decided that, apart from phoning each other regularly, we would continue to write to each other – but this time letters, instead of postcards, for, as Josh pointed out, he did not want the postman knowing our private business.

My Darling Kate,
Well, where did that holiday go? I only spoke to you this morning but I can't get you out of my head. Have looked at my timetable and it is pretty full I'm afraid, so unfortunately don't think I'll get home before Christmas – will keep ringing and writing when I can. How's the flat? Hope you are not too lonely without me. Did you buy that double bed we saw in the sales? I hope so. Just try to imagine my arms around you, my darling, when you're under the duvet every night, holding you close. Loving you forever, Josh xxxx

Darling Josh,

It will seem such a long term without seeing you. The flat is great but living over the shop means I'm always on call. Took me ages to get home from London yesterday, leaves on the line or something, so got back in the dark, didn't like that much – anyway, shouldn't moan should I? I did buy the bed, it looks and feels great, loads of room! I will have to hug a hot water bottle until you get here, with your nice warm feet! Loving you too forever, Kate xxxx

PS Just bought a naughty little black nightie, can't wait to show you!

CHAPTER 11 – FUTURE DREAMS

Willow Green Village Hall was full to the brim with revellers in various modes of fancy dress, who had gathered to mark the arrival of 2005. I was there, thoroughly enjoying the festivities with Josh, Ben, and his fabulous new girlfriend, who I knew very well – very well indeed. I cannot tell you how excited I was to discover he and Beth had started dating. I considered them a handsome couple as they smooched around the floor to a slow song, hardly moving amidst the crush of people. The raucous party eventually ended and everyone went their merry ways; Josh and I staggered arm in arm back to my flat. We had not realised how late it was until the church clock began to strike the hour.

"Two o'clock, better get in quick," Joshua quipped, "don't want to meet any walking dead, do we?"

"What made you say that?" I mused.

"No reason. You're not scared – are youuu …?" He retorted, attempting a creepy voice.

"Of course I'm not; the dead don't frighten me," I responded truthfully. He looked at me, puzzled for a minute and then threw his head back and laughed. With the full moon shining brightly in the clear night sky, we reached the arched entrance to the church, where Josh gathered me in his arms.

"Darling Kate, I do love you. There's something I've wanted to ask you for ages and I can't think of a more romantic time or setting – Kate Oliver, will you marry me?"

***

We lay in bed until almost midday making plans for our future together. I could not believe, after all my dreaming I was at last going to be Mrs. Bannerman. Of course, our wedding would not be for at least a year, as we still had six months until we finished uni, but after that, a forever future stretched out in front of us.

Everyone was overjoyed at our news – well, nearly everyone. Father threw us an impromptu party at the farm for family and friends – most were able to come, even with the short notice, the notable exception being mother. Why should I have been surprised, that even after all this time, she would be so uncaring? She sent a text message though, wishing us well. A text. My own mother sent a text.

By June, with immense relief, we eventually reached the end of three long years of dedicated study and exams. On the first Sunday after graduating, Beth and I were busy in my flat cooking a roast beef dinner; the boys had made some feeble excuse about too many cooks and had just popped down the pub.

"I think the four of us going on holiday is a great idea Beth, how good of your grandparents to let us have their bungalow for a week," I said as I tried frantically to rescue the gravy from its lumpy consistency. "So, how's it going – with you and Ben, I mean?" Beth looked dreamily out of the kitchen window.

"Ben? Ben, he's wonderful, he's so ..." she

drooled.

"If you're about to tell me my brother's a good lover," I cried, "I'd rather not know."

"Good! He's ..."

"Thank you, Beth ..."

I really didn't want her to finish her sentence, because I didn't want to be haunted by the vision of my friend and my brother making mad passionate love, however I did relish the reality that they seemed happy – if possible, as happy as Josh and me. The sound of the boys returning soon reached our ears, so we served up the four full plates of roast beef with all the trimmings – delicious, even if I do say so myself.

***

A few weeks later, the narrow, winding country road taking us on upwards towards the bungalow seemed everlasting; thankfully, Beth was familiar with the route so tackled the drive without any hesitation in her smart, brand new Ford Escort – an unexpected gift bought for her by her doting grandparents when they found out she had gained her degree. Reaching our destination, we all decided categorically it had been well worth the climb.

"Wow, take a look at that view," I exclaimed, looking wildly all around me. "I'm sure I can see the sea."

"Not quite," mused Beth, "but it is breath-taking, I've always loved coming here for family holidays. Let's get in and unpack, then I'll give you a guided tour."

Allowing the boys to struggle with our suitcases, Beth quickly unlocked the heavy front door, the portal to Valley View. "My grandparents have just had it redecorated, so excuse the smell of paint fumes; perhaps it might be a good idea to open a few windows."

While Beth and I ran from room to room letting in the summer air, I began to embrace our surroundings. Although the walls had been freshly painted, giving the whole place a nice clean feel, the furniture, I reflected, looked a bit antiquated.

"Thought you'd like this bedroom, it's the only one with a double bed," Beth pointed out as she pushed open the bedroom door, revealing a metal-framed double bed, adorned with an old-fashioned floral throw.

Following a makeshift dinner, a compilation of tins from the kitchen cupboards, we sat in the walled garden for a while discussing our plans for the week. We unanimously decided that as the weather was so amazingly hot, the beach at Bude would be our first port of call. Tired from our journey, and following a couple or more large glasses of white wine, we eventually went to our respective bedrooms. Ben and Beth took the one nearest the front door, from where I definitely heard the scraping sound of beds being pushed together.

Snuggling down between the crisp cotton sheets, Josh began to kiss me tenderly. With his mouth moving down my naked, yearning body, pleasuring every crevice, I pursed my lips to suppress the scream of ecstasy that was longing to erupt from my very core.

"I love you so much, Kate," Josh whispered, sometime later as I lay in his arms following our vigorous lovemaking. Taking my left hand, he stroked it gently. "As soon as we get home let's go shopping for an engagement ring; diamond, I think." A diamond, I told him, would be perfect. Ultimately, we fell into a deep, peaceful slumber, completely content in our happiness.

The following morning we were all up early, eager to enjoy our holiday. "Definitely going to be another hot day, just heard the weather forecast," disclosed Ben, emerging dripping wet from the bathroom, shortly followed by a slightly embarrassed Beth in a bright pink towel.

"Good, let's hope it lasts all week. Did you leave some hot water for us?" I teased, causing Beth's blushes to deepen.

After a meagre breakfast of toast and coffee, we took the short drive to Bude. The beach was already becoming crowded as we claimed our space on the fine hot yellow sand. It was a beautiful spot in a kind of sheltered cove; large pools of water were dotted here and there, an irresistible enticement for children and grown-ups alike. Although the sea was some distance away, we could quite clearly hear the sounds of the roaring waves crashing onto the golden beach.

"Can you rub some suntan lotion on my back, please Josh?"

"It will be a pleasure," he assured me, delighted to have an excuse to touch me again – and I was certainly not going to complain.

"Don't you two ever stop?" groaned Beth. "There are other people on the beach you know, or are you so much in love you haven't noticed?"

"Come here, old grumpy pants, I'll rub some in for you," exclaimed Ben, taking charge of the lotion. We lay there sunbathing for about an hour, until the boys decided they were bored and wanted to explore the area.

"Coming?" invited Josh. I turned to look at Beth who seemed quite comfortable where she was.

"A bit later perhaps, give us girls time to chat."

I watched as the boys weaved their way through the hordes of excited holidaymakers, before I leisurely lay back on my towel. I think I must have just fallen asleep, a dangerous thing to do in the midday sun, when unexpectedly the blast of the Life Guard's siren boomed out along the shoreline. Beth and I sat up immediately at this ominous haunting sound, trying to see what exactly was going on, bewildered by the scores of people now running and screaming for bathers to get out of the water.

"Wonder what all the fuss is about?" remarked Beth, clambering to her feet. Staring out in the direction of the sea, to my immediate relief I could see Ben and Josh running towards us. Josh was smiling broadly – he even raised his hand and waved while mouthing he loved me. Shading my straining eyes from the strong sunlight, I turned to Beth.

"There they are, soon find out what the problem is." When I turned back, Ben came more into focus, but as his features grew nearer I perceived the stricken look of horror on his face; the look of complete despair. Where was Josh? I pondered; he was there a minute ago.

"Kate, oh Kate, I'm so sorry," he howled, tears pouring down his sunburned cheeks. "It's Josh, the bloody wave took him, took him under, there was nothing I could do. I'm so sorry," he repeated again and again, as he held me tightly to his chest. What was he talking about? I had just seen Josh; I had just seen the man I love waving and smiling at me.

Rising rapidly from the depths of my very soul, came a terrifying scream. "No! Please no!" I wailed, before collapsing into a heap upon the sand as the realisation hit me that, yes, I had in fact seen Josh – but as only I could see him, from beyond the living world.

A traumatised Ben, choking with emotion, eventually tried to explain how my beloved had disappeared from his sight. "It was all my fault, it was my decision to walk on further, but the beach just got narrower and the rocks ... then it happened, a bloody wave caught us, I was able to keep my balance but Josh." Beth put her arm around my brother as he struggled with his words. There was no easy way for him to explain; put simply, the sea had dragged his unwilling body forcibly into its violent swirl and then, in a blink of any eye, my lover was gone.

During the frantic hours that followed, the coast guard did everything they could to find his body but by nightfall, they were forced to call off the search, saying they would resume in the first light of day. I was completely numb. Reluctantly, Ben and Beth guided me back to the car and the three of us set off for the bungalow.

"I must phone his parents. What should I say? How do I break the news that their son is dead?" I whimpered as I began shaking uncontrollably with the shock.

"I'll phone them, darling, don't worry," reassured Beth, trying to calm me, "and I think I'll also call you a doctor."

Josh's badly battered corpse was eventually washed up a mile from where it went in – finally released by its tormentor who had destroyed both our young lives in a split second.

A few painful weeks later, the church in Willow Green was full to capacity, the very church where only eight months earlier Josh had asked me to be his wife. How desolate life can be: just when you think you have it all planned out, it takes an irreversible turn. I truly believed I could never ever be happy again.

CHAPTER 12 – A WEDDING

Several years had now passed – desolate years devoid of love – and my only reminder of my darling Josh were his letters and postcards, now bound forever with a pale blue ribbon. While I stared absent-mindedly from the bedroom window of my flat, day-dreaming about how it had felt to lie with Josh, remembering the smooth touch of his skin and the sensual smell of his aftershave, a shrill voice jolted me back to the present and to the laborious job in hand. My best friend was almost giving up hope of ever turning me into a fashionable clotheshorse.

"You're not wearing that dress, Kate, surely; it's not very flattering," Beth urged, as I pulled out a further offering from my minuscule wardrobe of garments. "Keep in mind we're about to see people who we haven't laid eyes on for years, we definitely want to make a good impression, don't you think?"

Of course, she was right; she was always right. It was she who had gone to such great lengths to organise our school reunion, sending out invitations far and wide. How she had managed to find time to do this and look after my tiny nephew as well was quite beyond me. I could not have been happier when she married Ben and then, to add to the icing on the already pretty perfect cake, along came baby Christopher ten months later, with his chubby cheeks and irresistible grin.

Their wedding had been an almost regal affair;

even our estranged mother, who father had finally divorced, citing her adultery with Uncle Jack, had managed an appearance on the arm of her amorous lover. I have to admit she looked quite striking in an outfit of navy and white, topped off with a fashionable wide-brimmed hat that must have cost a fortune. Fortunately, father was not to be outdone, as a Mrs. Veronica Jordan (known to us now as Ronny), a young blonde widow who, unbeknown to us he had apparently been seeing for some time, floated alongside him in a vision of turquoise. Shortly after the wedding, she moved herself and her meagre possessions into Hill Farm, much to Flo's understandable irritation as she had become accustomed to running the house her way, without any interference, for such a long time.

Mother's face was quite a picture of disapproval when she first set eyes on Ronny (I would like to believe she was a little jealous too but perhaps that is going a bit too far). Her obvious displeasure continued further when father introduced his new love to Uncle Jack who, true to form, seemed to drool with pleasure at the young pert woman being presented in front of him.

Anyway, apart from the awkward moments with my parents, it was a perfect, balmy June day – Beth looked absolutely stunning and had even managed to lose weight enough to squeeze into a size 12. My dress, in a taupe silk material (for Beth had insisted I was a bridesmaid alongside her older sister Emma), complimented her elaborately embroidered beaded ivory dress impeccably.

I had not seen Emma for some time because she had moved to France with her French husband,

Henri, some years before, but I felt a strong urge to engage in conversation with her when the opportunity arose, which it did once the formal ceremony was over.

"Doesn't Beth look fantastic?" I began, while we stood amongst the neatly tended gravestones of Willow Green Church, waiting patiently to be called for the inevitable photos.

Grinning broadly, Emma proudly declared, "Can't believe she looks so good; when she was younger she didn't stop eating. I'm really happy for them both." She gave me a friendly kiss and squeeze – I was taken aback slightly by this unanticipated, overly-familiar gesture from someone I barely knew.

"How are you enjoying living in France?" I asked, trying to look unfazed by her behaviour, realising that probably she had grown accustomed to the French way of showing affection. "I always intended going there myself one day. I used to have a French au pair – Gabrielle, Gabrielle Bayne – who disappeared unexpectedly from my life when I was very little, I often think of her." The face of Gabrielle entered my thoughts once more; I had never given up hope of finding her again. Perhaps with everyone around me settling down, now was the time to try.

Emma looked thoughtful for a minute, "That name rings a bell for some reason ... I seem to remember seeing it somewhere ... it will come back to me, I'm sure. You must come over and visit; I would love to show you around, and perhaps we could try and find your Gabrielle," Emma replied with enthusiasm.

"Yes," I affirmed, "I would love to," realising she would probably forget this impulsive invitation as soon as the wedding was over.

Father had arranged for a substantial marquee to be erected in the large garden at Hill Farm for the two hundred guests and five-piece live band, whose music rocked thunderously through the air, encouraging everyone, young and old, to join in the celebrations. It was agreed it was the best wedding reception held in the village for years. I even enjoyed the inevitable flirtatious attention from the young men, most of whom were friends of Ben, which being a bridesmaid brought. Drinks flowed freely, with some taking full advantage of father's and the Forrester family's generosity – notably Uncle Jack, who downed glass after glass of spirits at an alarming rate. Towards the end of the evening, regrettably, he managed to corner me in the house, out of mother's hearing.

"Little Katy, how are you?" He slurred as he tried to peer down my dress, taking in an eyeful that he obviously approved of. He had not changed, this despicable being – but I had. As a consequence of all the troubled events I had endured in my life, I had been gradually gaining an inner strength, enabling me to be more positive about myself and I was dammed if I was going to take any further offensive behaviour this low life thought he could continue to get away with behind mother's back.

"Get lost, you creep," I ordered, turning the tables and looking him up and down. "You disgust me, with your beer belly and bad breath; crawl back to my mother, you deserve each other!" An evil smirk filled his craggy features as he leaned in towards me, his face almost touching mine.

"I know ... I know lots and lots of secrets ... little Katy ..." he hissed, his words becoming distorted as he swayed ungainly from side to side, before the fast-approaching sound of my mother's clicking heels could clearly be heard on the wooden floorboards, followed by the urgent tone in her elevated voice, stopping him in his tracks.

"Jack, we're off, the taxi's here!" She screeched.

Watching my mother and her intoxicated lover climb in an ungainly fashion into their waiting taxi, I pondered on his pronouncement. Secrets; every family, I am sure, has secrets. I for one have many secrets, which my own family are unaware of – I contemplated for a brief moment on what he could possibly be hinting at. Whatever his problem was, I was not going to let his remarks get to me; who was he anyway, but a nasty bit of mess you'd find under your shoe? He truly repulsed me and I prayed our paths would never have to cross again. Sadly, realistically, I knew my prayers were in vain.

Following their week's honeymoon, Ben and Beth came home to take up residence in Farm Cottage, which had been left vacant ever since Jack's departure. Now they had a home of their own, a love nest, which father had spent money on to bring it up to date – he had even had a two-storey extension added on the side.

It was also about this time that Ronny moved into Hill Farm. I had nothing against her per se, she was a lot younger than father (probably in her mid-thirties, which meant she was only ten years older than I was) and I am sure quite pretty under all the make-up; she obviously made him happy, what more could Ben and I wish for him?

"Keeps trying to tell me how to suck eggs," moaned Flo during one of our Friday meetings. "I've been housekeeper for your family, Kate, for almost thirty years, who does she think she is, telling me how to manage the house!" Poor Flo, I think she was worried her services wouldn't be required for much longer, now Ben and I had both flown the nest. With this new young female in residence, would father recommend the unthinkable; would he suggest Flo retired?

CHAPTER 13 – NEW BEGINNINGS

Beth and Ben's wedding had happened last year, now we had a school reunion to plan.

"Thank god for Facebook, without it I wouldn't have been able to contact so many people. How many replies is that now, Kate?"

With an inevitable outcome I could not evade – the fact I now had to go shopping for a new dress – Beth had finally turned her attention away from my disastrous wardrobe to how many former pupils would be attending the centenary anniversary reunion of Willow Green Primary School.

"One hundred and twenty at the last count, including guests. Look, we've even had a reply from Louise Turley: says she and her new husband, Brett Miller, are looking forward to attending; great, we'll have a celebrity in our midst."

Louise had certainly made her mark since moving away. Almost overnight, she had become a very sought-after glamour model for a national newspaper, before marrying a first division footballer, Kevin Blackmore. The pair were never out of the limelight, unfortunately usually for the wrong reasons, which was for either drunken behaviour or their hostile fighting in public places.

Unsurprisingly, the marriage did not last and, following a large settlement granted to Louise, they divorced in the full glare of the media. Not one to let the grass grow under her feet, she soon remarried, but not before throwing in her modelling career. With the money she received from selling her story, she set up a donkey sanctuary somewhere in the Midlands. I know all this mind-numbing information because, I have to admit, I read trashy magazines.

"Had the unfortunate experience of bumping into Barbara Hamilton last week who seemed to think her husband would definitely be attending, alongside her adoring son, who will be honouring us with his presence all the way from South Africa," Beth informed me, before continuing, "Never really understood what happened there."

No, neither did I. One minute Stephen was working, supposedly successfully, in London; the next minute his parents were seeing him off on a plane from Heathrow airport, bound for Johannesburg, without any explanation to the local gossips and he had not been home since, as far as I was aware. So our gathering was becoming quite an elite affair, with an ex-glamour model, a supposedly highflying financier, his father – our former Headmaster, Charles Hamilton, who since his retirement had become a bit of a recluse – and, oh yes, I smiled to myself, a spiritualist medium whose abilities had yet to be exposed to the outside world.

***

A few days later, the village post office, now my full time place of work, was packed with pensioners collecting their weekly pensions. As had become the norm, I was dealing with the Tuesday rush and Laura was busying herself filling the shelves with produce, when PC Robinson entered for his daily tea and chat.

James had recently become our local bobby and, because he had been born in Willow Green, was on first name terms with all the locals.

"Morning Laura, it's a nice one again." His dark, handsome presence always caused her to giggle like an infatuated schoolgirl.

"Morning James, I'll just pop the kettle on. Do you want tea Kate?" she called over to me, as I commenced counting out Patricia Wood's money. I nodded my head in acknowledgement.

"Good looking young man, that," Patricia Wood pointed out, "surprised he's not been snapped up; you don't think he's gay, do you?" she whispered through the glass partition. The possibility of James being gay had never entered my head. However, she was right, he was certainly gorgeous. I even recalled having a crush on him at school. With the morning rush having subsided, James and Laura re-emerged from the stock room at the rear of the shop.

Sidling up to me, James cleared his throat. "Kate, got my invitation yesterday to the school reunion, just hope I can get that evening off. I wondered ..." he hesitated before continuing, "I wondered if you would come with me as my ... date?"

I was taken aback. It had never dawned on me that James might fancy me. I had to think quickly; I did not want to dismiss his offer but, there again, I had not been out much since ... since Josh. Perhaps it was time, a little voice was telling me, time to look to the future. I suddenly felt decisive.

"Thanks James, I'd love to go with you, but that's some way off yet, how about going out one evening this week?" Over his shoulder, I could see the broadening smile on Laura's face, which said it all – I was finally back from my self-inflicted isolation.

The likelihood of James being gay kept running around my head when we met at the Bull on Thursday night, but not before I had had to endure a complete Beth-inspired makeover.

"You have a lovely olive complexion, Kate, you don't need much skin make-up," she pointed out, dabbing my face gently with a small sponge, the surface of which was coated with the latest foundation. Beth applied tones of gold and brown shadow to my eyelids, with the intention of accentuating my dark brown eyes. I glanced in the mirror. I could not remember the last time I wore so much make-up; I hoped it was not too much. With further help from Beth, I chose a sleeveless red dress and, with my black hair released from its stretchy band, at last I was ready for my first date with James.

On hindsight, perhaps our local pub was not the best choice for our rendezvous, mainly because of all the inquisitive eyes and the knowing looks that followed us as we entered the heaving tavern. James purchased our drinks and immediately we took them into the quieter small bar away from the main hubbub. We sat there for at least five minutes in silence, supping occasionally at the cool liquids in front of us, until James eventually instigated the conversation.

"You do look stunning Kate, red really suits you – you should wear the colour more often." He smiled warmly as he gently brushed a stray strand of hair away from my face; in doing so, he stroked my cheek lightly with his hand. Unexpectedly, I felt aroused by his touch. "I can't tell you how long I have wanted to ask you out, the time never seemed right, Josh was a good friend of mine," he lowered his head.

"I loved Josh very much, but he's gone. I'm glad I'm here tonight with you, James – I'm sure he would approve." I took his hand in mine and held it tightly to reassure him that we were not being disloyal. We sat chatting for ages, until, before we knew it, the landlord was calling time. On this occasion, he took my hand as we stepped out into the warm evening air to begin a leisurely stroll along the twisting cobbled paths of our village, happy and content in each other's company. Reaching the door to my flat, I turned to him. "Do you fancy a coffee?" I proposed, eager for him to say yes.

He looked at me apologetically. "I'm sorry, I would really love to but I'm on early shift tomorrow morning. Perhaps another time?"

I cannot tell you how disappointed I felt but, before he turned to go, he leaned forward and kissed me tenderly on my lips. I was aware of my whole body yearning for his caress, but it was not to be. Watching him walk away from me in the moonlight, I decided I definitely wanted to see more of this handsome, gentle man, who I truly believed had the capability to mend my broken heart.

Later, climbing into my empty bed, I felt a strong spiritual presence had entered my room. Unexpectedly, from out of nowhere, the enchanting tune that normally erupted from my jewellery box drifted around the walls, growing louder as its journey progressed. Eventually, as slowly as it had commenced, the sound faded away. Leaving the warmth of my crumpled bed, I removed my perfect trinket box from its safe place in my wardrobe. Carefully lifting the lid, the tiny ballerina began her graceful dance to the now familiar melody. What was she trying to tell me?

The following week, James took me out to dinner to a very romantic Italian restaurant in town. The food and his company were wonderful and this time when I asked if he wanted to come up for a coffee, he did not turn me down. Sprawling out on my settee, loosening his tie and kicking off his shoes as he did so, my heart began pounding hard in my chest.

"Sorry it's only instant," I pointed out, emerging from the kitchen. He took the hot mug carefully from me and set it on the table, as I manoeuvred myself next to him. "That was a lovely meal, have you been there before?" I asked, suddenly feeling embarrassed at the situation I had initiated.

"Only once, for a birthday celebration, though I didn't enjoy it as much as I did tonight. Kate, you know you are really beautiful."

He pulled me gently towards him, until our mouths came together in a long, lingering embrace, while his hand began to caress my breast before moving slowly towards my back, where it carefully unzipped my dress. The costume fell unashamedly from my shoulders, exposing my strapless bra. His tongue and lips continued their search of my now half-naked body. With our emotions heightened, I led him enthusiastically to the comfort of my double bed. Rapidly removing our remaining clothes, our pleasure increased as we explored the intimate areas of every part of each other, before our eager bodies finally came together in an explosive act, which seemed to give us both enormous satisfaction. James was certainly an unselfish lover, bringing me to a climax of sexual gratification that I did not know was possible.

He definitely was all man – twice, in fact, that night!

***

The next day in the post office, Laura was intrigued as to the outcome of our date; actually, everyone in the village seemed to be aware of our dinner engagement, of course I only disclosed part of my evening to the throngs of people who were interested – the finale to our encounter was certainly not for public debate.

The time for the school reunion was now looming fast, and familiar faces were beginning to arrive in our normally peaceful village, causing a huge buzz amongst the locals. Unfortunately, the excitement that should have been exuding from every quarter was unexpectedly brought to an abrupt halt due to the carefully addressed manila envelopes which began mysteriously dropping through certain letterboxes. The said correspondence, bringing their intended recipients a great deal of distress with the incriminating words that had been meticulously written on the paper within – words penned by a troubled writer with high moral ethics which they could no longer suppress.

CHAPTER 14 – LOUISE

Louise Elizabeth Turley was born on the wrong side of the sheets and the shame of her arrival was a reality her distraught Catholic grandmother was unable to accept. Immediately after she took her first breath, she and her teenage mother were flung out of the council house Brenda had lived in all her life, onto the streets of Manchester, before the neighbours had a chance to hear the cries of the tiny new-born. Brenda never saw or spoke to her family again, knowing she had brought such disgrace upon them. Louise's father? Well, Brenda was unsure who he was but she hoped he was Andy, the son of the local publican. Alas, it could have been her cousin Frank, who used to stay over and creep into her room at night, when everyone was sleeping. His assaults began on her fifteenth birthday and, as she lay there whimpering into her pillow, he had whispered into her ear that nobody would believe her because this is what women were put on the earth for – as if that made it right. Yes, she hoped her baby was Andy's; at least he told her he loved her as they made out in the dark shadows of the narrow alleyway, only fifty yards from her front door.

Brenda and her baby stayed for a time in temporary accommodation, full of homeless mothers. In this confined setting, there was a continuous fight for survival and never any peace, either from crying babies or squabbling individuals, who were all vying for the use of the meagre facilities. Relief came eventually in the form of a social worker, who managed to find her a place of her own: a two-bedroomed flat in a high-rise complex well away from all she knew. The view from the large floor-to-ceiling window was wonderful, but that was all that was wonderful. They lived there for almost four years, amongst the filthy hallways and lifts (which were frequently out of action), until one day, a junkie set fire to the building, bringing chaos for the council's housing department.

"I'm sorry, we have very little to offer you unless, of course, you would like to try out of the area?" the smartly dressed housing officer sighed apologetically. Consequently, that is how they moved to the village of Willow Green, their only possessions just two small suitcases of second-hand clothes.

Flo was the first one to welcome Brenda and Louise to the village. Being her next-door neighbour, she quickly realised she couldn't avoid contact with the single mum, who villagers had already decided was a loose woman and should be kept at arm's length, and definitely well away from their husbands. Fortunately, they got on famously and Flo soon became a surrogate mother and grandmother, which fulfilled both their empty lives. Louise was always knocking on her door asking to play, and Flo loved having the curly-haired child around. They would chat endlessly and Flo would tell her about Kate and her life on the farm. Of course, to a little girl who had nothing but the bare essentials, jealousy soon reared its ugly head, so by the time Louise started school she already had a preconception of Kate and had decided she hated the very ground she walked on.

By the time she had reached puberty, Louise had become conscious of the fact that she was turning into a very powerful female amongst the male population, as her body had grown and developed to the envy of other girls. The local boys found her irresistible, pursuing her around the village like dogs on heat. Of course, Brenda soon recognised her daughter was exceptional and did all she could to keep her away from the evil clutches of her many admirers. Unfortunately, Louise only had eyes for one young man, who was a little older than she was and, when he finally set eyes on her, did not need much coaxing.

Stephen Hamilton first noticed this voluptuous, leggy, blonde-haired girl as he backed his battered car out of his parents' driveway one afternoon. Slowly, he rolled down the window and flicked his cigarette out onto the path right at Louise's feet.

"Do you mind," she scowled, "there are laws about littering, pick it up!" She was used to boys jumping at her demands, but not this one; not Stephen Hamilton. He opened his car door and stood tall in front of her, eyeing her, approvingly, up and down.

"Fancy a spin?" he proposed confidently. Louise quivered with sheer pleasure at this rich boy who was obviously lusting after her.

"Sorry," she began, "my mum told me not to get into strangers' cars," and with that she turned and walked away, wiggling her hips a little bit more than usual, knowing he was watching. Stephen did survey her as she walked away, vowing to himself that this local strumpet would be his very soon.

An opportunity arose a week later as he was

driving home from school. Louise had missed the school bus because she had been kept behind on detention, and was now making her way along the lanes. Pulling up next to her, he opened the passenger door, and this time she jumped in.

"Thought you didn't accept lifts from strangers?" he smirked.

"Well you're not exactly a stranger now, are you? And anyway, I've seen you several times around school, you're in the sixth form, aren't you?" She asked, taking out her compact from her school bag to check her hair and make-up.

"Very good, ten out of ten for observation, go to the top of the class. Got chucked out of my last school, bit of a come-down having to come back here, but I'll survive."

He slowed the car and pulled it over to the side of the road, prior to unbuckling his seatbelt. His arm encased her shoulders as he leaned over and kissed her ardently on the lips. At first, Louise pushed him away, not wanting him to think she was easy, but then his hands began to fondle her body and, in the end, she found his advances hard to resist.

Of course, she was not adverse to boys touching her; she quite liked the feeling of excitement that being caressed brought her, and the power she felt over male emotions. She recalled going to the pictures with a boy called James, who got over-excited when his wandering hands found her breasts and, in his eagerness, he managed to knock his drink all over himself and the man sitting next to him, causing quick a furore.

"Let's get in the back, we will be more comfortable," he coaxed. Once in the back seat,

Stephen slid his hand up her inner thigh, eager to feel the warm space beyond.

"Stephen," Louise panted, "I've never gone as far as this before; I'm scared, I don't want to get pregnant." He stopped briefly and laughed.

"Don't you know you can't get pregnant the first time? You silly girl, now take off your knickers and let me in; you know you want it."

Traumatised by the whole experience, Louise quickly dressed herself and combed her tangled hair; her saving grace, she believed, was she was now the girlfriend of a rich boy, which meant she would want for nothing. How naive was her thinking.

Stephen drove her to the end of her road and as she stepped from his vehicle, she smiled back at him.

"When will I see you again?" she asked, eager for a positive response from the boy who had just taken her virginity.

"I'll ring you … soon," he promised, before roaring away triumphantly from his latest conquest.

Of course, he did not ring; in fact he made a special effort to avoid her whenever possible. Louise was heartbroken and she vowed never to let a boy make her feel that way again.

***

Months later, winter had gripped the whole country and the first fall of snow had covered the countryside in a white blanket.

"Are you skipping breakfast again Louise? You should have something, it's so cold outside," Brenda pointed out, concerned that lately her daughter was looking a little peaky.

"Don't fuss mum, I'll grab something in the cafeteria."

How could she tell her mum that not only could she not face breakfast, but that anything she ate only stayed in her stomach briefly; she had checked the calendar, she was definitely late. Her mum would kill her – pregnant at fifteen just like she had been. She had to contact Stephen; when he knew there was a baby on the way, his baby, he would marry her after her sixteenth birthday and put everything right.

Just after Christmas, she stood outside the Manor House, which, like the rest of the village, was enveloped in a heavy frost, waiting for him to emerge. At last, her patience was rewarded. Jumping in front of his vehicle, he had no option but to offer her the warmth of his car. They drove out of the village to a quiet spot off the beaten track. Stephen was hopeful for a repeat performance of their sexual encounter, but it was not to be.

"I have to talk to you, please stop …" she implored, pushing him away, much to his annoyance. She had imagined this scene over and over again in her head. She would tell him she was pregnant, he would say he loved her and the baby and they would be married as soon as possible. Of course, that is not exactly how it went.

"Stephen, I'm pregnant," she blurted out. Reeling from this revelation, he sat back in his seat staring out far in front of him.

"So … you're not trying to tell me it's mine, for fuck's sake. You're not telling me there haven't been others; after all, you are the village bike." He turned his head and looked at her; a vile expression covered his distorted face. "No, you're not pinning this on me," and with that he jumped out of the car, removed a cigarette from his pocket and lit it. Louise was devastated and leaped out after him.

"Why are you talking to me like that? I have never been with anyone else, never. You have to put this right, you have to marry me!" she screamed pulling at his coat.

"Marry you! I would rather gouge my eyes out. Get rid of it you stupid bitch or find some other sucker!" With that, he raised his arm and struck the wailing girl hard across her face before climbing back into his car and fleeing the scene.

***

Louise managed to hide her pregnancy over the weeks that followed, even from her mother, to whom she still could not bring herself to divulge the awful truth, for she truly believed she would never forgive her. In the end, she did not have to.

It was a Friday, the beginning of spring, and Brenda was out at one of her meetings. Louise, feeling exceptionally tired, had taken herself off to bed early when the pains started. She ignored them at first, but then slowly they became unbearable. On the way to the bathroom, she had an uncontrollable urge to push down. While she lay in agony curled up on the bathroom floor, a sea of blood surrounding her, her tiny son came silently into the world.

He was so very small; he never really stood a chance. Instinct took over as she cut the cord with an old pair of scissors, before wrapping him in a towel – tears were now tumbling uncontrollably from her eyes. Carefully, she carried him through the house and out into the garden as panic rose in her. What the hell should she do now? She had no option but to get rid of him, of course, because no one must know about her sin. Just at that moment, the moon appeared from behind the clouds, illuminating the structure at the bottom of the garden.

"I'm so sorry," she whispered into the little bundle before letting slip the tiny mite from her grasp. She watched regretfully as his lifeless form tumbled from her arms into the bottomless well.

Although feeling weak from the loss of blood, she had no choice but to clean the bathroom before eventually returning to her bed. She was still feeling exceptionally poorly the next morning but managed to rise, before her mother materialised, in order to attend the Saturday morning doctor's surgery. Before she could say anything, Doctor Daniels knew at once there was something very wrong with Louise.

"Doctor, you won't tell my mum, will you?" she pleaded as he began his examination.

"I took an oath Louise; I do believe your mother should be told but, no, she won't hear it from me. How far gone do you think you were?"

"About ten weeks, I think, when I lost it I got scared and flushed the toilet, it was horrible." She closed her eyes tightly, hoping the good doctor believed her story and could not tell by examining her that the baby had been, in fact, almost six months old. He did not reveal whether he believed her or not, instead he took out a prescription pad from his drawer.

"I'll give you a prescription to help you with the discomfort; you need to rest completely for the next few days."

Thanking him for his time, she turned and left the room, whereupon he began to write up her record notes. He pondered for a moment before entering the age of the foetus as 'unknown'.

***

All this happened years ago, and what a life she had led since then. Back briefly in her mother's house, she was surprised to receive an unsigned letter, the contents of which sent a cold chill down her spine.

BABY MURDERER – Sinner confess, I know your secret.
Confess or I WILL TELL ALL.

So, who else knows about the baby? Obviously, she realised, someone in the village does, as she stared at the carefully written words. Holding the paper tightly in her grasp, she vowed to herself that she would never reveal her secret, not after all these years; too many people would be hurt. Her new husband, for one, would never understand. No, she would not allow anyone to destroy her marriage, or the new life growing in her belly.

She held the paper carefully over a lighted candle and watched as the unwelcome words disintegrated before her eyes.

CHAPTER 15 - REVELATIONS

"Must you go to your book club meeting this Friday? I've hardly seen you this week."

I laughed warmly at the sight of this grown man, naked in my bed, pleading with me with his puppy dog eyes.

"I told you James, it's been planned for weeks. I can't let the girls down at the last minute."

For the first time I really wanted to tell him the truth; wanted to include him in that part of my life. However, I was afraid; afraid he would judge me insane, not all there, out of my trolley, whatever he might call it and more importantly, I was afraid he would leave me – just when I was falling in love with him.

"So, come on then, what book have you been reading? I've never seen you looking at anything else but magazines," he joked as he grabbed me and pushed me back down onto the bed.

What could I say? My mind was in a whirl.

"Doesn't the policeman in you ever stop?" I quipped.

"You know what they say: once a copper, always a copper. Come on answer my question, the name of the book?" I eased myself off the bed and turned my back to him. "Kate, your silence is making me feel uneasy; you're not reading a pornographic novel are you? Is that why you won't tell me? If you are, believe me, I won't be shocked."

I made a rash decision: if he was the man for me, it was probably best he knew now rather than years down the line. I turned and looked at this wonderful man staring at me with understanding and acceptance in his eyes, perhaps for the last time.

"James ... I believe in life after death, in fact ... I'm a medium; I have seen and can talk to those who have passed over to the spirit world. There! I've said it; if you want to walk away I'll understand."

James rose slowly to his feet. "I see, and why would you think I would want to leave you; do you think I'm that shallow? Let me tell you something," he began softly as he took me in his arms, "You might be surprised to learn that I have first-hand experience of spiritualism: my own mother, like you, was a medium, so you see, I understand only too well."

Being able to share my secret with James, and his reaction, was such a relief it overwhelmed me, so much so that I began to weep on his shoulder.

***

Friday night arrived and we gathered at Laura's cottage, to prepare them, I had already pre-warned my friends: I was bringing a surprise guest to our meeting. James's presence certainly caused a stir in the beginning but, after we had reassured everyone that he was not averse to our gathering, the group soon settled down. I was more than a little nervous, at first, with my boyfriend in the room as I took prime position in the circle. I still had very little control over my contact with the other side, so I was not too hopeful of any successful encounters this evening, until, that is, a mist encased the room and effortlessly I was lifted onto another plane.

I could see a familiar figure in front of me: Brenda's twin sister, Beryl, was beckoning me to follow her. Eventually she stopped and turned to face me, and I could see a small bundle in her arms, which she held out to me. I tried hard to make out what she was holding but, just as I got near, she and the bundle faded from my eyes.

However, the spirit world had not quite finished with me yet, for the next thing I knew I found myself once again on the village green by the willow trees, a familiar place where several of my encounters had occurred. From a distance, I could see someone playing hide-and-seek amongst the draping branches.

"Come over here, Kate, I want to talk to you," the apparition indicated as I glided over to the soothing voice that seemed to have hallucinogenic powers. "Kate, my name is Sarah and I've come here to warn you, my dear, to beware, someone …" she seemed to look about her as if afraid of being overhead, "wants to hurt you …" and with that she vanished and I found myself back in Laura's cottage.

"Wow! That was different; I'm not sure what it was all about," I confessed, before relating some of my experience to the group. I decided not to share the bit about the warning, as it had shaken me rather, and I was not sure how to deal with the revelation – I needed time to think it over. We all tried to analyse the rest of the manifestation without much success, although I could not help but notice Brenda was unusually quiet; perhaps she understood the motive behind her sister's appearance, but for some reason did not want to disclose her interpretation to us. Of course, it was her prerogative, if that was the case.

With our main meeting over, we sat chatting together for a while.

"How's the organising going for the reunion, Kate?" asked Emily, "I hear you're looking for any old photographs of the school." She leaned down and reached into her bag. "I've been searching the attic at the rectory and found an old album, which must have been up there since before the First World War. It's full of pictures that must go back to the early life of the school. I've brought it with me if you would like to take a look at it." Carefully, she removed the dilapidated book and placed it on the coffee table.

"What a fantastic find, I wonder if there's any photos of my grandmother; her family arrived in the village around that time," Flo pointed out as she began sifting through the historical pictures. All of us found it truly fascinating, scanning the old prints and scrutinising the eager faces of the children, who were now sadly long gone.

Sometime later, as we stepped out into the night air, James took my hand in his. "Do you mind if we just pop back to mine? I could do with some clean clothes."

Up until now, I had not been to James' flat, which he shared with another police officer, whose beat was in the next village. Straight away, you could tell men lived there – the whole place oozed masculinity.

"Sorry about the mess," he apologised, moving several layers of clothes off the chair to enable me to sit down. "Won't be a minute."

Being left on my own, I had a quick snoop around. There were very few personal items of the two occupants about the place, apart from a couple of photos on the old sideboard. I picked up the larger of the two frames and immediately came face-to-face with the spirit I had just encountered.

"That's my mother, when she was younger, of course," exclaimed James proudly as he re-entered the room. Perceiving the startled look on my face he continued, "Is there something wrong?"

"Your mother ... you didn't tell me she had died," I began, "was her name Sarah?"

James took a deep, emotional breath. "She died several years ago of cancer. How ... did you see her tonight?"

"Yes, I didn't say anything because she gave me a warning which disturbed me and I didn't want to distress everyone else as well."

"Shit!" James put his hands on his head and started to walk swiftly around the room.

"I'm so sorry if it's upset you," I cried. We sat talking together for hours about his mother and the warning she had given me, while holding each other tightly for comfort. I finally felt a strong bond had cemented our relationship. Whatever the future held for us, if we had a future together that is, I knew I would always cherish him with all my heart.

CHAPTER 16 – THE HAMILTONS

"A teacher must always be on guard and never find themselves in a compromising position with a student. Many a career has been destroyed by misinterpretation of a good deed."

Thought-provoking words, which Charles Hamilton remembered throughout his illustrious career. He recalled the day clearly when he was called into the headmaster's office, following a complaint from an irate mother, whose son had told her that Mr. Hamilton had kept him after school, purportedly for extra English, and had abused his powers by touching him inappropriately. Of course, it was the boy's word against his – thankfully, for Charles, the situation was resolved amicably before it became public knowledge. Unfortunately, the outcome was that both the headmaster and the governors deemed it best all round if Charles left quickly, without any fuss, and seek employment elsewhere – for his own sake.

Being out of work for a while gave him time to reflect: if he was to stay in education perhaps he should marry, to reinforce his status as a heterosexual – as far as the outside world would perceive, anyway. Up until this point in his life he had been a very private person and the social scene had never held much interest for him, but now he decided it was time to spread his wings, perhaps even frequent his local pub – at least, he convinced himself, it was a start.

He first noticed Barbara when she and a group of friends were drinking in a quiet part of the bar. It took all his courage to ask this rather plain, mousey-haired woman if he could buy her a drink, quite expecting her to laugh in his face; therefore, he was more than a bit surprised when she accepted his offer. Their relationship progressed quickly, as time was not on either of their sides and, within a year, not only had they become engaged but they had also become man and wife. Barbara had been brought up in a moneyed family, so from the very beginning of their marriage they were lucky enough to be mortgage-free.

Apart from the first few weeks of their married life, when Charles tried his best to overcome his aversion to intercourse with a woman in order to please his new wife in the bedroom department, their sexual relationship was, well, to be frank, almost non-existent. That was the reason a frustrated Barbara turned her energies towards the advancement of her husband's career. Her reward came swiftly when Charles was offered the position of Headmaster at Willow Green Primary School – he accepted the post without hesitation. Furthermore, she managed to find them her dream home, in the form of the Manor House, which she believed created the right image for their up-and-coming pivotal role amongst the village community.

Barbara was soon in her element, volunteering for every committee going, until at last she achieved her goal of becoming chair of the local WI. Following her landslide election, being the only candidate, she decided they just had to throw a garden party.

She loved the organisation of, as she perceived it, the main social event of the year. "The garden and the house need a lot of work before we can open it up to the villagers, I don't think I'll have time to do it all myself, Charles," she announced one morning over the breakfast table, "what do you think about hiring a gardener or odd-job man?"

Sighing over his wife's latest proposed extravagances in spending his hard-earned money, he folded the morning paper carefully and rose from his chair before replying. "That's fine with me, dear." In truth, he had always hated gardening and his DIY skills were practically non-existent, so having someone around who could do all these things seemed, after he had had time to mull the idea over, an excellent suggestion.

The following week, a postcard appeared in the post office window advertising for a handyman for the Manor House. There was only one reply: Harold Devine, Flo's husband, who at this time was in his forties and actually quite attractive in a weather-beaten sort of way.

"So, Mr. Devine, are you an experienced handyman?" she cringed at her opening question, not having had much practice of her interview technique.

"Oh yes, Mrs. Hamilton, I have several other jobs as handyman in the village, including Doctor Daniels, who I am sure would provide me with a reference."

Having had no other replies to her advert, Barbara realised she really had no alternative but to hire Harold. Fortunately, he proved a very good worker and in no time, the house and garden had undergone an elegant and colourful transformation. The day of the garden party arrived and, as her home filled with inquisitive eyes, Barbara felt relaxed in the knowledge that everything around her had been honed to perfection.

Following the success of the event, they decided that Harold should remain in their employ – his presence keeping everyone happy. Charles, for instance, realised that his wife would no longer nag him about mowing the lawn or cleaning out the gutters. Whereas Barbara, well, she liked the smell of pheromone that Harold emitted on those hot, sweaty summer days. It was on one of those days when, as she watched him from the patio window removing his shirt, showing her his well-developed middle-aged male form, she could not help but be aware of a stirring in her loins. She had given up totally the hope of ever having a proper relationship with Charles; in fact, they had had separate bedrooms for several months now.

"Do you fancy a cool drink?" she called to Harold, who was busy planting the begonias he had so lovingly grown from seed. He nodded in her direction and immediately put down his trowel. "Come in out of the heat, it must be nearly thirty degrees out there, don't want you passing out." She handed him the cooling glass of freshly-squeezed lemonade and, as she did so, she brushed his hand gently with her finger. Their eyes met for a brief moment before he handed her back the empty glass.

"Thank you, Mrs. Hamilton, well, must get back to work, them begonias won't plant themselves you know."

The months rolled by and as far as people on the outside were aware, Charles and Barbara had a good marriage; she was always by his side supporting him at school events and he in turn helped her when it came to anything to do with the WI. Yes, they both knew how to put on an act. Therefore, it was with some surprise when one day, without any explanation, Charles announced he was going away for the weekend and would not be able to help her collect the jumble from around the village. She would cope, she knew that, but the question in her mind was: why the mystery – why would he not tell her where he was going?

The very moment his car drew away from their drive, she immediately began a search of his bedroom. Right, Charles Hamilton, she thought to herself, time to find out exactly who you are. Normally she did not dare enter his domain, respecting his privacy, but today ...

Everything in the room was so tidy; even his wardrobe was immaculate with rows of carefully-stacked shoe boxes, dominating the right hand side. Just as she had given up hope of ever finding anything, she happened to notice she had inadvertently moved one of the boxes out of sync. Not wanting to leave any incriminating evidence of her intrusion, she reached into the closet to straighten it and, in doing so, clumsily knocked several other boxes to the floor. From out of the rectangular containers tumbled, not shoes, but magazines and pictures of naked men in erotic poses. She had speculated, of course, that Charles was gay; they had never talked about it, but deep down she knew and her find only confirmed this. She had tried to convince herself that despite his obvious reluctance to indulge in the sexual side of their relationship, she could live with that – she believed strongly she could make their marriage work, and anyway, to be honest, she had always thought that sex was very much overrated. However, her biggest sorrow was that she would never become a mother; never know the love of her own child.

She was on her second bottle of red wine when Harold called round later that evening for his wages.

"Come in Harold, please, your wages are in the kitchen."

Realising at once she was a little worse for wear, he entered the long, impressive, dimly lit hallway, albeit a little reluctantly.

"Oh by the way," she slurred, "while you're here, could you look at the tap in the en-suite? It keeps dripping."

Without waiting for a response from him, she began to climb the grey-carpeted, snaking stairs and he had no other option but to follow at her heels. "Charles is away this weekend," she volunteered, "otherwise," she chuckled, "I'm sure he would have been man enough to deal with it."

She led him into her bedroom and quietly pulled the door closed behind them. Unaware of the situation he had found himself, Harold carried out a swift examination in the en-suite.

"Can't see any problems with the tap, Mrs. Hamilton, but I'll get my tools and change the washer just to be sure."

He turned around, with the full intention of exiting the room but, unfortunately for Harold, Barbara had other ideas. Already having partly removed her clothes, she pressed her whole body up against his and began to kiss him eagerly.

"Mrs. Hamilton, I'm a married man and you're, well, I don't think Mr. Hamilton …"

"Don't you fancy me, Harold? Come on, I won't

tell anyone – it'll be our little secret."

She began to unbutton his shirt, kissing his chest with her impatient lips, as the fastenings fell away from his torso – he did not try to stop her. Eagerly, her hand slid purposely down into his trousers until, finally, he could no longer resist her advances. Once their clothes dropped onto the bedroom floor, their animal instincts took over, coming together in a loveless embrace just to satisfy their need for sexual gratification.

Over the next few weeks they had several silent encounters in different parts of the house, from which they both found complete satisfaction, that is, until Barbara realised her dream had come true: she was pregnant – so she no longer needed Harold, to whom selfishly she never divulged the reason for her ending their brief affair.

She remembered clearly the day she told Charles about the baby: he did not even look away from the documentary he was watching on the television.

"Of course we'll bring it up as ours, if you agree, Charles."

"Fine with me, dear," he responded with surprisingly no emotion.

Stephen Hamilton came screaming into existence on a chilly morning in May and at once became the centre of his mother's world. He wanted for nothing. Regrettably, the outcome of being spoilt caused him to become so obnoxious from an early age that even Barbara craved distance from him from time to time. Consequently, she decided to employ an au pair. Actually, over the years that followed, a succession of au pairs took up residence in the Manor House; not too surprisingly they never seemed to want to stay long.

When he reached five years old, Barbara insisted they sent him to a private school.

"I don't think it would be a good idea for him to go to your school, Charles; people might think you'll give him preferential treatment."

Charles rolled his eyes at his wife's suggestion. He had tried to like the boy for Barbara's sake; he had never blamed her for finding affection from another man – after all, he had, on many occasions. He did love her, though, in his own fashion, especially the way she seemed to accept him as he was but, try as he might, he felt no love for Stephen.

By the age of thirteen, Stephen had been expelled from three different schools; of course, it was never his fault. The holidays were the worst time for his exasperated parents, for then he would creep out of the house early and not return until dusk. The truth was he had created a den by the river, after stumbling across the derelict metal construction one day, beneath mounds of overgrown vegetation.

It had taken him days of hard graft to reach it and then several more to clear out the dilapidated interior to create his secret hideaway, the headquarters for his gang of three boys from the neighbouring village who had collectively made the decision to be soldiers when they grew up. Of course, Stephen had nominated himself as captain and had subsequently laid down the rules for the rest of the troop to follow.

Their favourite pastime was daring each other to steal; not big things, just the odd sweets or caps for their guns, but their greatest excitement came from nicking fruit from orchards. On one particular day, they had all clambered over a moss-covered, high red brick wall before propelling themselves into the garden beyond, only to be confronted by an angry old soldier, Alfred Reed, who managed to trick them into entering his garden shed where he confined them until the police arrived.

The police sergeant decided to teach the boys a lesson by locking them briefly in the cells at the station. All the parents were shocked to find out about their behaviour, when they arrived to retrieve their repentant sons, and forthwith grounded them for the rest of the school holidays.

At least, three of them were repentant; Stephen decided there and then he wanted retribution for the loss of his freedom and he took it a few months later. He had planned his revenge carefully, observing Alfred from afar, learning his movements like a soldier in a war studying the enemy. He learnt he went to the pub in the next village every Friday night to play in the darts team, and religiously propped his old bike up against the pub wall.

One Friday in November, he took the spanner he had previously stolen from Harold's toolbox and followed Alfred to the pub, where, endeavouring not to be observed, he began the task of loosening the nuts and bolts on the wheels of Alfred's pushbike. His task completed, he slunk back into the shadows of the night and watched with growing anticipation as the elderly gentleman wheeled his pushbike towards the road, before mounting it carefully and commencing his trek homeward along the dark twisting lanes. Stephen jogged along behind him at a safe distance, waiting with growing anticipation for the wheel to be released from its whining, rusting body.

He was beginning to think he had not loosened it enough when at last his patience was rewarded: from around a particularly sharp bend, a car's startling headlights approached them rapidly, causing Alfred to swerve, whereupon he lost control and was catapulted into a frozen, shallow ditch. Swiftly arriving at the scene, Stephen peered down into the dark incline at the crumpled pensioner, so cruelly sent to his grave.

Striding away triumphantly, his steps now lighter with the knowledge he had taken the revenge he had been craving for so long, he smiled the smile of an assassin – who was still only fourteen years old.

***

Stephen had always believed he got away with it; in fact over the years he had put the incident so far back into his mind, it was as if it had never happened. Returning to England, after a plea from his mother, following his temporary exile – the outcome of unproven accusations of sexual assaults on women at his place of work – he was rather taken aback when he opened the envelope so carefully addressed to him.

MURDERER – Vile creature I know what you did.
Confess or I WILL TELL ALL.

He had no choice, of course, but to seek out the sender and deal with the bastard in the appropriate manner.

CHAPTER 17 – OBSESSIONS

"I'm so sorry, Kate, this cold has really knocked me for six," Beth wailed as she croaked and sneezed down the phone. "Is there someone else you could ask to go with you? I really think you need a second opinion before you buy anything."

Poor, darling Beth; a cold was the last thing she needed at such a crucial time ahead of the school reunion.

"Don't worry, I'll ask James if he'll come with me, just take yourself back to bed and don't forget to drink lots of honey and lemon, my nan swears by it, and make sure my brother takes care of you."

I put down the receiver with a sigh. I had really been relying heavily on Beth to advise me over the purchase of a new outfit, especially since she had made it perfectly clear she regarded my fashion sense as practically non-existent. Fortunately, for me, James was very pleased to be asked to accompany me, making it apparent he loved the atmosphere London brought to a shopping expedition.

Wednesday was our early closing day in the post office and James's day off, so with my credit card carefully positioned safely in my handbag, wondering if it would actually see the light of day, we caught the one o'clock train to embark on our shopping bonanza.

Surprisingly, although it was the middle of the week, Oxford Street was buzzing with eager shoppers jostling for bargains amongst this minefield of consumerism. Of course, it did not take me long for my enthusiasm to wane and for my poor feet to let me know they had had enough, thank you.

"Just one more store," pleaded James, "then we'll have something to eat and drink. Beth won't forgive me if we go home without anything, after all, this is the fashion capital of the world; if you can't get what you're looking for here, then it doesn't exist."

If I did not know him as well as I did, this remark would have made me rethink my beliefs about his sexuality, as it certainly brought to the fore the female side of his character.

Stepping through the revolving doors of Selfridges, my spirits lifted, for we had finally reached my favourite department store in the whole of London. I remember my father bringing Ben and me every Christmas when we were young, to stare in awe at the twinkling festive lights but, I have no doubt about it, the pinnacle of our trip was definitely a visit to Selfridges Santa, who I believed lived in the most magical grotto imaginable. The place still felt truly special to me and, with this renewed zeal, we continued our search.

"Hey, how about this, I recollect red really suits you," remarked James, holding up a shimmering number.

"I couldn't wear that," I shrieked. "I'd be too conscious of falling out. And then I'd need shoes and a bag …"

"Just try it on for me, please," James coaxed.

Reluctantly, I took the item into the changing rooms, determined I was going to hate it. Obviously hoping for a sale, an enthusiastic shop assistant handed me a pair of red sling backs to try on with the ensemble. Annoyingly, they all fitted perfectly and as I gazed at my reflection in the long mirror, I secretly admitted to myself that this garment, which was now gently hugging my body, actually made me feel a tad glamorous. Emerging nervously from the changing room, the shop assistant enthused on how wonderful I looked.

"Wow!" exclaimed James proudly, "you look amazing – you really do," and with that he leant towards me and kissed me lovingly, bringing a rosy colour to my cheeks.

I looked down at the tag; was I really about to part with £225 on a dress I was probably only going to wear once? The answer categorically was definitely yes. Now I had a multitude of shopping bags to carry and with my ordeal finally at an end, we began to look around for somewhere to eat – of course, so was everyone else. Luckily enough, we eventually found a table in the corner of Pizza Hut and, with relief, we sat down.

"I think you'll be the most glamorous woman there on Saturday," declared James, as if he felt I needed further reassurance.

"I very much doubt that." I smiled. "Don't forget Louise will be there, I'm sure every man's eyes will be firmly on her." James shuffled in his chair as if weighing up whether or not to tell me something. Eventually, he took a deep breath and, without looking at me, began his pent-up confession.

"I went out on a date with her once … to the cinema." Poor James, I wondered how long he had wanted to tell me that.

"I see, so you were one of her groupies." I joked,

almost choking on the slice of pizza out of which I had just taken a large bite.

"Ok, make fun. Like most of the guys in the village, I was bowled over by her, hmm ... outer beauty. Anyway, I obviously wasn't her type!"

No, I thought to myself, but the sicko Stephen Hamilton was.

"Lucky for me then," I grinned, before continuing, "did I tell you that Mr. Hamilton, our old headmaster, has agreed to attend? Haven't seen him out and about in Willow Green for years."

James went quiet for a minute before contributing.

"Couldn't stand him, he was a creep. He was constantly offering to give me extra tuition after school. Thank god mum didn't like him either and refused to let me stay. I don't think he was too happy about it and was quite persistent, told my mum he expected great things from me if she would only let him coach me, but she would not give in. The rumour going round at that time amongst the boys was he was queer and on hindsight that wouldn't surprise me, he always seemed to find an excuse to come into the boys changing rooms and ogle."

"I remember hearing something along those lines about him from my brother. If Mr. Hamilton makes a pass at you at the reunion, you can arrest him." I beamed.

Leaving behind the streets of London, which were now jam packed with theatre-goers, I put my arm through James's and, lifted by our day, we walked briskly towards the underground.

***

The following morning, I was not too surprised when Laura handed me a letter with a French postmark, addressed to me. I could see from her face she was bursting with curiosity about its contents, but I decided to wait until my lunch break to open it.

Now, the post office had always been the centre for the local people to catch up with each other, namely any gossip that was circumnavigating the village at the time was discussed in depth on its premises. I tried hard not to either eavesdrop, or be cajoled, into conversations about my neighbours and friends which would cause any of them an upset. Today, however, word had finally surfaced concerning the poisoned pen letters.

Who had started the rumour, no one was sure; perhaps someone who had received the unwanted correspondence had let slip about its arrival, but gossip was now rife in this small community of ours. Of course, the focus was on who was sending them, and why? Everyone, including Flo, was reluctant to point a finger at a potential culprit, perhaps just in case they too became a recipient. Nevertheless, everyone agreed that the time had come for the police to be informed and, as the girlfriend of the local bobby, I was unanimously elected to be the one to convey this speculative information. Reluctantly, I agreed to bring the subject up with James when I next saw him.

Before Flo left the shop, she took me to one side. "Kate dear, I won't be at our next meeting … its Harold." As Flo's eyes welled up with tears, I led her to the stock room out of sight of inquisitive customers. "It's his heart, he only told me this morning, apparently he's known for months but he only told me, his wife, this morning." I put my arms around the woman who had been more than a mother to me than my own, and hugged her, not wanting to let go.

"I'm so sorry, Flo, is there anything I can do? You know you've only got to ask." Flo wiped her eyes and smiled a watery smile.

"There's nothing anyone can do, apparently; it's inoperable, it's just a matter of time. Anyway, I must go, I want to treat him to something nice for dinner." I watched Flo with a heavy heart as she turned away from me; with her head bowed, she walked out of the shop.

Lunchtime at last. Up in my flat with a cheese and pickle sandwich situated alongside a steaming mug of tea, I tore open the envelope. I had already guessed it was from Emma, as Beth had told me she had spoken to her recently about the fact she couldn't make it to the reunion, and during their conversation Emma had divulged to Beth that she had written to me. It was an invitation, as she had promised, to visit her sometime in the very near future. She informed me she had uncovered some information about Gabrielle she thought I would be very interested in, but she wanted to show me and not simply explain it in a letter and that all would be revealed when I stayed with her in the next few weeks. I found all this cloak-and-dagger stuff intriguing – very intriguing indeed.

CHAPTER 18 – WHEN JONATHAN MET ROSEMARY

Jonathan Oliver was born at Hill Farm, and was the second son of Tom and Victoria Oliver. The Oliver's had almost given up hope of ever having further children until his arrival, mainly because their eldest son, Tom Jr., was already sixteen. Sadly, their happiness was short lived, when Tom Jr. died unexpectedly from a brain tumour. His mother never recovered from his brother's sudden death and, sorry to say, never really bonded with Jonathan. On the other hand, from almost the minute Jonathan took his first steps, his father realised that at last he had a son who had the passion for the soil as he did and was not afraid of a day's hard graft. Jonathan thoroughly enjoyed his childhood, working alongside his father at every opportunity, whilst listening intently to his visions for the future of their land.

By the time he had left school at eighteen, he had enrolled on a Farm Management course, which also opened up his social life, propelling him into a new scene of parties and girls, who found his rugged good looks hard to resist – the women were literally falling at his feet. One of the first females who caught his eye was much older than he was and definitely not a virgin.

He took Sharon for a drink one evening to a small intimate village pub and, from the beginning of their date, she made it obvious to him that she was definitely out for a good time. Flaunting her curvaceous body in front of him, he found his eyes immediately drawn to her low cut t-shirt, which looked warm and inviting to the young, eager farmer. They left well before closing time and walked slowly along the canal path, taking them around the long route towards her parent's house. The sultry evening air and the star-filled sky created a perfect night for romance.

Continuing to amble along the uneven path, they came upon a gnarled bench nestling, hardly visible, amongst the riverside vegetation. Sharon was the first to stop and quickly took her place on the wooden seat, before motioning for him to join her. Now, for all his manly good looks, the truth was Jonathan had had little sexual experience with women, apart from the odd snog and grope in the back row of the cinema, and he certainly had never encountered a female as forward as Sharon – but that was without doubt about to change.

Pressing hard up against him, he could feel her breasts bearing down upon his chest, bringing him heightening pleasure. While his eager hands began to explore the shapely body before him, she began to remove her clothes and his. He stopped for just a moment to admire the sight of her exquisite, milky-white form, which even in the dim twilight was clearly visible. Then, without so much as a word, she straddled his manhood, rising and writhing until they both exploded with pure ecstasy.

An hour later, as he left her at her ivy-covered front door, he told her he would call her, knowing full well he had no intention of seeing her again. However, their encounter seemed to open up a floodgate of longing within him; a strong craving to have further sexual encounters with as many of the opposite sex as he could. In other words, he became a ladies' man and his conquests surprisingly loved him for it, even his male friends became a little jealous of his tales of his sexual exploits.

By the time he was twenty-three, Jonathan was practically running the farm single-handed because his father was now full of arthritis, and on a good day could only manage a trip around the fields in his jeep, just to check everything was in order. His mother, well, she had fallen into a deep depression and now hardly left her bedroom, from where she ate and slept alone. Doctor Daniels tried to persuade the family to put the poor woman in an institution but Tom would have none of it, instead he hired a nurse to address her every need. It was no surprise, therefore, to any of the villagers – in fact, most agreed it was a blessing – when eventually they heard the news of her passing. There were only a few mourners at the ceremony and afterwards her wooden and brass coffin was laid as she had requested, beside her beloved first-born son.

With his mother no longer around, Jonathan began to bring his numerous girlfriends home on a regular basis. His father turned a blind eye to his carryings-on, appearing to accept his son's behaviour as long as the farm was being run to his satisfaction – he believed Jonathan deserved a private life, albeit one of debauchery.

***

Rosemary Weston had a much humbler beginning, having been born on a north London council estate.

Being a headstrong teenager, inevitably she got herself into bad company, and before she was sixteen-and-a-half, found herself unofficially engaged to a local hoodlum. She kept her fiancé hidden away from her parents because she knew that they would not approve of the union and would probably have chucked her out of their terraced home. At about this time, her father Stan was given a big promotion at work, which not only meant an increase in income for the family but also a move south, in order for him to manage a newly opened branch of his firm's car factory.

The thought of relocating out of London threw Rosemary into a complete meltdown. She shrieked at her parents, Stan and Sylvia, that she categorically would not go and they could not make her. Of course, in the end she was dragged along with them, screaming and shouting that she hated the ground they walked on, they were ruining her life and she would kill them in their sleep!

Years later, Stan and Sylvia agreed, they had probably saved their only daughter from a life of self-destruction, when she eventually emerged from a business course with outstanding qualifications. Fortuitously, Rosemary immediately managed to secure herself a job in a high street bank, the very bank where the Oliver family kept their accounts. Consequently, Jonathan and Rosemary's first meeting was through the bank's glass partition.

Love (if you would like to call it that) was not instant; in fact, Jonathan hardly paid attention to the young female eagerly batting her eyelashes at him from the other side of the counter. For it had not taken Rosemary long to realise, after finding herself in a position of trust, that she could easily search through the accounts of all the wealthy unmarried men in the area for a potential husband. Therefore, when she first set her eyes on the tall, handsome and – on paper – rich Jonathan Oliver, she made up her mind there and then that he was the one, and at once began to put together a plan to lure him into her honey trap.

Their first encounter outside the walls of the bank happened on a very wet Thursday afternoon. The heavens had just opened up to a deluge of rain and hail, which soon began flowing rapidly along the gullies of the street, looking for the many outlets that were inevitably blocked. Rosemary was on her lunch break, with her umbrella now unceremoniously blown inside out, when she slipped quietly into the café, dripping from head to toe. In the far corner, his head firmly in a farm magazine sat Jonathan – Rosemary knew he was here, because she had secretly watched him enter the place from the upstairs window of the bank.

"Mr. Oliver, fancy seeing you here." Jonathan looked up at once, a blank expression on his face. "It's Rosemary … from the bank, do you mind if I join you?" she asked coyly.

Jonathan quickly scanned the drenched beauty standing in front of him; he instantly perceived her erect nipples, which could clearly be seen through her soaked, white lacy blouse. How could he turn her away?

Two weeks later, they 'bumped' into each other again. She was waiting for a bus and he was driving past in his Land Rover; seeing her standing there with her long legs hardly covered by a short denim skirt, he slowed and offered her a lift. This time they made a date to see each other the following Saturday.

Rosemary had done her homework on Jonathan, found out that he was a philanderer, and had even managed to talk to some former girlfriends of his in order to find out more about him. So, when he predictably suggested going back to the farm for a 'nightcap' she declined his invitation, kissed him goodnight and left him wanting her – oh, how he wanted her.

Weeks went by and miraculously Rosemary had managed to keep Jonathan at arm's length, until one evening in July when they had been out with friends and were sitting outside her parent's cottage, kissing goodnight.

"Oh Rosy, your skin is so soft," exclaimed Jonathan feverishly, as he began to kiss her bare shoulders. Gradually his mouth moved to her breasts, Rosemary was beginning to realise that she could no longer stop herself, for this moment at least, she needed him almost as much as he needed her. Perhaps the time was ripe.

"Shall we go on to somewhere else?" she suggested temptingly.

"The farm?" he replied, eager to fulfil the need that was building up inside him.

"No, not the farm, it should be somewhere special, a hotel perhaps?"

They drove for about half an hour before they arrived at a quaint bed and breakfast, with a vacancy sign hanging in the netted bay window. The lady owner showed them into a newly-decorated room, dominated by a large queen-sized bed, adorned with a gold silk throw.

"Breakfast is from six-thirty a.m. until nine a.m.," she informed them before handing Jonathan the key, "sleep well," and with a knowing look, left the room.

Falling into each other's arms, they began to remove their clothes enthusiastically. "Shit, I forgot to bring a condom," panted a frustrated Jonathan. Carefully, Rosemary reached into her handbag.

"My mum always taught me to be prepared," she grinned, handing him the packet that had been waiting patiently for its party piece. Smiling with anticipation, she lay back on the large bed, waiting for the moment her future husband would enter her for the first time, unknowingly using one of the packets of condoms she had carefully pierced that morning, in order for his sperm to impregnate her.

So it was, that Jonathan Oliver (an extremely reluctant bridegroom) did the honourable thing and married Rosemary Western (a conniving gold-digger bride) in a quiet, intimate ceremony in September of that same year, watched over by her relieved parents and his ailing father, who sadly did not survive long enough to meet his grandchildren.

***

Now many years later and divorced from Jonathan, Rosemary was more than a little upset when a manila envelope arrived on the doormat one morning, at her bungalow in Dorset. Screaming hysterically for Jack to come quickly, the words written by the poisoned pen writer jumped out at her from the paper.

MURDERER.
Confess to your crime so the dead can rest in

peace.
Confess or I WILL TELL ALL.

Her mind racing with wrath, she scanned the barely visible postmark on the envelope: yes, there was no doubt at all, it definitely read 'Willow Green'. Hastily throwing a couple of suitcases into the boot of their car, she and Jack headed out directly to find and take care of its sender.

CHAPTER 19 – 'LIME HOUSE'

"Well you seem a lot better than you did yesterday." I beamed at my best friend, who now at least had managed to progress from her bed to the sofa.

"Yes, my temperature's down at last," Beth announced, relieved, taking a sip from the lemon drink I had prepared for her. "You've just missed Ben; he's taken Christopher out for a bit of fresh air. Been a great help, my husband has and so, by the way, has Ronny."

"Oh yes, is that a jibe at me? I do have to work, you know," I reminded her, "and it was your idea, if you remember to go and buy an outfit for Saturday."

"Don't get upset, at least you've got something to wear. I'm sure you'll look fabulous," Beth coaxed. "Come on, what's the gossip from the post office? Any more news on those poisoned pen letters?"

I had to admit there was nothing more to report. I had my own theories though on the matter, including the fact that probably not all the recipients were going to admit to receiving one – mainly because there was possibly some truth in the carefully scripted words. Of course no one, not even me, knew that in between the accusations of stealing, animal cruelty, and adultery, were some amongst us who were actually being accused of murder – no, those individuals would be foolish to admit to receiving those unsolicited correspondence, wouldn't they?

Friday morning dawned, the day before the school

reunion, and I was busy getting ready for work whilst at the same time planning the evening in front of me. Because James was on a late shift, we had arranged to meet up later for a light supper cooked by yours truly, when I thought it would be an ideal opportunity to approach the subject of the poisoned pen letters. Then, without warning, someone began banging on my front door.

To say I was stunned by the appearance of my mother at the threshold of my flat would be an understatement, for in the four years or so since I had lived there, she had visited me on only two occasions. The first, after she had come up from her love nest in Dorset specifically to see father and, once she had established he was not at the farm, began scouring the village like a woman possessed (I personally think he had advance warning of her visit and had disappeared on purpose to avoid another row with her over money). The second was when she was looking for somewhere to crash for the night, following a drunken fight at the pub, where she and Jack had unceremoniously been asked to leave. Therefore, in truth, mother had never actually visited in all these years just to find out about my welfare.

She seemed extremely agitated as she paced up and down my already well-worn carpet, before uttering a single word.

"Kate," she began (at least, I thought, she remembered my name). "You work in the post office … I spoke to Flo in the street yesterday; I hear there have been rumours of … nasty letters being received?"

"Nasty letters?" I repeated innocently.

"Yes, yes, nasty letters … you know the sort, sent

maliciously to upset people. Well, do you?"

Of course, I knew about the letters, but I was a little surprised she was so uptight about them, unless of course she had received one herself … yes, yes, of course, that was why she was here; my mother was being accused of a crime of some sort. Would she tell me or would I have to guess about its contents? Was it about how cruel she had always been to me, or her affair with Jack? No, her affair was all out in the open and anyway she had moved away with him years ago. So, was it about me?

"Well …" I began, not wanting to give too much away too soon. "Yes, there has been talk of a poisoned pen letter writer in the village, but I haven't actually seen anything they have written, have you received one then?" I blurted out, before stopping to think. Clenching her fists tightly, turning her knuckles white, she spun around and glared at me.

"I wouldn't be here if I hadn't – would I? Has anyone any idea who has been sending them?" she hissed.

Wow, she was truly in a state. Calmly, I sat down and crossed my legs before replying, my relaxed demeanour causing her further agitation.

"There has been some speculation amongst the villagers, but no; no prime suspect yet. I think, though, it obviously must be someone who knows the locals well," I swallowed hard before I uttered my next words. "What did the letter accuse you of then?" She looked at me with eyes of pure evil.

"Tax avoidance … yes, they accused me of not paying my taxes." I did not believe her, of course; no one would be in the state that she was over not paying her taxes. Finally turning to leave, she added,

"If you hear anything, anything at all, Jack and I are staying at the pub for a few days."

Before I opened the door, keen to see her go, the shrill sound of my phone filled the air and then my answer machine kicked in for us both to hear the message so clearly being conveyed. It was Doctor Daniels, informing me his housekeeper had found some pictures from his school days at Willow Green Primary, and if I would like to borrow them for the reunion, I could pick them up this evening. I made a grab for the receiver before he rang off, to tell him I would drop in after work about six o'clock, that is, if I managed to catch the five forty-five bus. His voice seemed to have composed mother's frame of mind and she actually smiled a thoughtful smile as we parted.

***

It was a slow day in the post office, until a face from my past strutted confidently through its door. Louise looked beautiful, even though she was dressed casually in an old pair of jeans and t-shirt. She made a beeline for me, straight away grabbing my shoulders and planting a wet kiss on both cheeks.

"Wow, mum said you still worked here, how are you keeping?" I felt a sense of sympathy in her tone. As we began to delve into each other's lives, it brought to the surface how boring and predictable my own had become. Without really thinking it through, I brought up the subject of the poisoned pen letters, just to bring a little colour to the conversation.

"Have you heard about the letters? They've certainly spiced up the gossip around here." The expression on Louise's face changed immediately.

"Letters? No, I've not heard about any letters," she imparted in a defensive manner, taking me rather by surprise. Just then, Barbara Hamilton appeared from behind the dried goods shelf.

"Oh yes, my dear, they are causing quite a stir in the village. Why even Stephen got one himself yesterday morning; don't know what it said, but put him in a hell of a bad mood. He stormed out of the house and we haven't seen him since. Mr. Hamilton and I are very worried about him."

This declaration from the mother of a sex maniac caused a knowing look to pass between Louise and myself, thankfully putting an end to what had become an uncomfortable conversation between us. I watched in awe as she glided from my sight, speculating that perhaps the poor girl had in fact received a letter herself. What possible revelations could the evil writer have to disclose about Louise that had not already been put into print?

Five-thirty at last. While Laura turned the 'open' sign on the door, I rushed upstairs to get my cardigan before setting out for Doctor Daniels house, which lay in a small hamlet on the outskirts of the village. Glancing quickly around my bedroom for my elusive handbag, my eyes alighted on my latest purchase. Did I do the right thing? I pondered, not for the first time, as I gazed uncomfortably at the glittering red garment hanging majestically from my wardrobe door. I had no time to hesitate any further; grabbing my bag, I rapidly descended the outside steps from the flat and ran swiftly towards the bus stop.

Damn, I missed the hourly bus by two minutes. I did not have time to wait for the next one, and so had no alternative but to walk the mile and a half of country lane towards Lime House, the good doctor's dwelling. Recently I had made the monumental decision that it was about time I learnt to drive; in fact, I had already filled out a form to apply for my provisional driving licence and, in fact, Ben had said in one of his 'I love you sis' moments that he would teach me. However, that was in the future; now, I had no choice but to walk.

Thank goodness, the dark clouds that had haunted the day had completely dispersed, revealing a late spell of bright sunshine, which was now lighting my path. I had always loved this route, especially at this time of the year. The twisting road was edged by field after field of yellowing corn, now swaying gently to the rhythm of the light breeze, whilst wild multi-coloured flowers intermingled with tall grasses, encroached the overgrown hedges and hardly-visible footpath that I was at this moment confidently treading.

I had not set eyes on Doctor Daniels for quite a while, mainly because he had retired in recent years and had become a bit of a recluse. There had been a double-paged article in the local paper on his retirement, praising him for his dedication as a doctor to the surrounding villages. Several people had related stories of his commitment to their families; how he would come out in all weathers or hours of the day without complaining. The journalist also mentioned his patients never had to make appointments, it was simply first-come-first-served. On a negative slant, he did go on to comment about Doctor Daniels inept way of keeping his patients' records, which always seemed to be strewn around his desk, although the good doctor insisted he knew exactly where everything was.

The article had also included a photo of his wedding day, which had made me realise I had never been privileged to meet his wife, who had died several years before I was born. Apparently, they had two sons during their marriage, both of whom now lived in Canada. I thought at the time, when I read the piece, how sad it was that such a good man, who had devoted his life to others, would live the rest of his life alone in the house once filled with the laughter of his family.

Rounding the next corner, with relief the white wooden gates of Lime House came into view. Approaching the impressive entrance, I was almost knocked off my feet by a post office van overtaking me, its driver, Kevin, tooting enthusiastically in recognition (if only he had been a bit earlier, the idiot could have given me a lift, I fumed to myself through gritted teeth). The short walk along the unkempt, lawn-edged, gravel drive led me straight to the imposing black front door.

Without hesitation, I climbed the three stone steps and began reaching forward with the intention of ringing the antiquated bell, which hung motionless against the wall, until I realised that in fact the door was already slightly ajar.

I called out first before pushing the wooden entrance open, revealing a large red and blue tiled hallway, the centrepiece being a sweeping staircase rising proudly to the upper rooms in this magnificent Georgian residence.

"Doctor Daniels, its Kate, Kate Oliver, I've come for the photos," I cried again, striving to reveal my presence to whoever could hear me. My voice seemed to echo eerily along the walls and through the rooms of this cavernous dwelling.

From somewhere in the distance a door banged shut, followed by an unexpected cool breeze, causing goose bumps to erupt on my skin. I called out once more and then I plucked up courage and began to walk along the length of the passage. Still no acknowledgement of my presence, that is, until I was aware of the appearance of a figure someway in front of me.

Immediately I recognised the bent form of a now very elderly Doctor Daniels, who, without uttering a single word, beckoned me to follow him. He led me straight into a room, which I perceived at once must be the library as two of the walls were draped from floor to ceiling in books; a large desk monopolised the far corner, near to an opened window. I was instantly astonished at the spectacle in front of me: documents were scattered everywhere, whilst the air flowing from the garden was intensifying the disturbing mess.

"What's happened, Doctor Daniels? Have you been burgled?" I exclaimed apprehensively, before attempting to step over the numerous papers carpeting the wooden floor. Although I began to tread carefully, a white envelope attached itself to my shoe. Bending down to release it, I glanced at the name clearly written on the front: 'Kate Oliver'. Feeling the envelope, I supposed it contained the photos for the school reunion, so I stuffed it quickly into my handbag.

Then my eyes alighted on a disturbing sight – a pool of blood seeping from beneath the desk. Moving cautiously behind the dark wooden structure, to my horror I came upon a man's body.

"Doctor Daniels, who is he?" I cried, looking wildly around me for his assistance. Why would he not speak to me? "Doctor Daniels!" I repeated, desperate now for an answer from the man I had always held in high regard.

Still no response was forthcoming. I bent down to verify if the man lying so crumpled on the floor was, as I feared, in fact dead. Gently I pushed him over, in order to check his breathing, but as I completed the manoeuvre, my own breath was almost taken away from me. For the body lying so dramatically in his own blood was that of Doctor Daniels!

Cradling him tenderly in my arms and with tears now cascading unashamedly down my ashen cheeks, I rocked backwards and forwards, humming softly to the man who had been such a big part of my growing up. I realised, of course, his soul had already left his lifeless body – it was his spirit that had guided me here. I took a quick scan around the room to see if his spirit was still about. No, he had already disappeared.

In intense shock, I looked down at my clothes and hands, realising they were soaked in his blood. Before I could reach for the phone to call for help, a hysterical cry erupted behind me. Doctor Daniels housekeeper, Mrs. Norton, was slumped in the doorway, wailing frenziedly. Staggering to my feet, I began to take a step towards her, causing the poor woman to scream even louder, before warning me to stay away.

"Murderer!" she bawled, repeating the word again and again, before adding, "I've called the police." I dropped once again to the floor in complete despair. Surely, no one would believe I was capable of killing anyone.

I had found myself in a nightmare situation, from which I felt unable to wake; time seemed to have decelerated into slow motion, until moments later the urgent sound of sirens, created by several police cars and an ambulance, now travelling up the drive at high speed, reached my ears. Although strongly protesting my innocence to the numerous individuals eagerly gathering around me, no one seemed to be listening to my pleas.

I found it near impossible to comprehend what was actually happening and, as the metal handcuffs snapped shut, encasing my thin wrists, an officer in plain clothes began to read me my rights.

"Miss Kate Oliver, you have been arrested for murder. You do not have to say anything, however, it may harm your defence if you do not mention, when questioned, something which you later rely on in court. Anything you do say may be given in evidence." I began to sob and my nose began to run profusely.

Two burly police officers escorted me brusquely from Lime House. Walking side by side along the duration of the hall, we were not alone: the troubled spirit of Doctor Daniels, whose unexpected death had been so unnecessarily violent, appeared to me once more. His presence bringing me assurance of his acknowledgement of my innocence as my life spiralled to an all-time low.

CHAPTER 20 – FOUR GREY WALLS

The excruciating journey to the town of Dunwell, where the police headquarters for the surrounding villages was situated, seemed endless, until the driver swung a sharp left into the almost-full police station car park. Entering the red-bricked building, accompanied by my police escort, I soon found myself at the front desk and in the presence of the custody officer.

"Well, well, what have we here?" he enquired, his large build towering over me.

"Kate ... Oliver ..." I stuttered, trying hard not to cry.

"We arrested Miss Oliver at Lime House, sergeant, for the suspected murder of Doctor Daniels; she was read her rights at the scene," one of the officers declared.

"And I thought it was going to be a slow evening, Doctor Daniels was a great man," the custody officer sighed. "Miss Oliver, do you understand the charge?"

"Yes ... I understand but ..." What else could I say? What I wanted to do was shout and scream for the whole world to hear that I DID NOT DO IT!

"Miss Oliver, I need you to empty your pockets and remove your jewellery please; it will all be stored, for the time being, in a locker." I really was trying to keep it together, but as I watched my belongings being taken away from me, tears began to trickle off the end of my nose.

"Can I have a tissue, please?" I asked politely. Reaching beneath the desk, the custody officer produced a box of tissues. It proved quite difficult to blow my nose with my hands still in handcuffs.

"I think you can remove the handcuffs, Miller, I don't think Miss Oliver is liable to make a dash for it." I smiled a weak smile in recognition of his apparent understanding of my character. "I have a few forms for you to fill in, but first I need you to follow this female officer so you can remove the clothes you are wearing. They'll be needed for evidence."

Solemnly I followed the young officer to a side room, where I peeled off my blood-stained clothes, replacing them with a pair of grey trousers and a shirt, both of which were at least two sizes too big.

Returning to the front desk, the custody officer continued processing me with little emotion in his voice. "I would also point out you are entitled to legal aid, would you like me to contact the duty solicitor?"

Duty solicitor? I had to think fast. Yes, of course, I needed a solicitor but … "Hmm … I have a solicitor … Miss Brightman. I have her number in my address book, it's in my bag."

My handbag had been taken away from me at the house, after I had undergone a thorough search. Reunited with it, albeit for a brief moment, I quickly found my address book, which housed the mobile number for Molly Brightman, Ursula's friend. While the custody officer dialled for me, I wondered what reception I would receive from this eminent city lawyer, who I had not seen or spoken to for quite some time.

"Miss Brightman? I am the custody officer at

Dunwell Police Station. I have Miss Kate Oliver with me and she would like a word with you, I am passing the phone to her now."

Taking the phone, I tried to explain quickly to Molly the position I had found myself in. Of course, she was flabbergasted, not only to hear from me, after all this time, but more importantly the nature of my call.

"Kate, it is imperative that you don't say anything to anyone about what happened until I get there, do you understand? I will catch the first train I can and should be with you within two hours. Is there anything you want to ask me?" It was wonderful hearing a supportive voice, after all the negative vibes I had been feeling around me.

"Can I ask to phone anyone else?"

"Yes of course, you should have been told that. Look I'll see you soon, keep strong, now please pass me back to the custody officer." Molly obviously had a few sharp words to say to the custody officer before concluding the call, as his manner immediately changed towards me.

"Sounds like, Miss Oliver, you have friends in high places. Anyway, if you would like to call someone to let them know what's happened?"

Whom should I ring? My first thought of course was Flo, but she had so much on her plate just now – what with the worry of Harold – no, I felt I could not burden her any further with my problems. Father then, yes, I could phone father and he, in turn, would relay my predicament to Ben and Beth. My call to him was highly emotional. When I first heard his customary tuneful way of answering, I could not bring myself to speak – he even began to think I was a heavy breather, causing his mood to change traumatically as he started swearing at me from the other end of the line. When I eventually found my voice, it trembled with emotion down the receiver. Of course, he was devastated and wanted to come at once, but I had to tell him his journey would be in vain, as the custody officer said he would not be able to see me today anyway.

Still wearing the unflattering grey garments and with all the necessary legal procedures covered, which also included the humiliating process of taking my fingerprints and a swab from my mouth for DNA, I was led away down a maze of corridors to the cells. The heavy door slamming behind me, followed by the jingling sound of the key turning in the lock, brought me further anguish. Four grey walls were now the entirety of my world – my home for however long it would take to prove my innocence. I recalled the thoughts I had had only that morning, how my life had become boring – please give me back boring, I prayed.

Holding my head in my hands, I sat on the only piece of furniture available: a narrow bed fixed hard against one of the walls. I began to imagine all the would-be criminals who had languished here before me: did they have to stay here long before being released, or were they now serving a jail sentence in some awful prison miles away, and would I be joining them? God, I had to keep positive about the British justice system.

The clunk of the door hatch being slid rapidly across made me instantly look up, as an unrecognisable face on the other side, informed me that my father and brother had arrived in reception. I was thankful that father had not listened to the custody officer and had come anyway, for just knowing they were here brought me comfort. Several moments later, the liberating sound of the key opening the door once more caused me to leap to my feet.

"Your ... hmm, barrister's arrived," the police officer informed me. "Come this way, she's waiting for you in one of our interview rooms." Barrister? Well, well, well.

Molly Brightman looked striking with her auburn hair tied into a neat bun, and her navy blue pin-striped suit emphasising her tall, slim stature.

"Kate," she enthused, giving me an unprofessional hug, which I really appreciated. We sat down opposite each other at a table containing a jug of water and two glasses. Molly removed a pen and notebook from her leather briefcase and then looked me straight in the eyes. "Right, now you must tell me everything that has happened."

I began with the events that had taken place that morning, from mother's unexpected visit, Doctor Daniels phone call, concluding with the discovery of the doctor's body.

"Ok, so let me get this straight. Doctor Daniels called you on your house phone, that's why you visited him today."

"Yes, mother heard him too; he had some old photos for me."

"Your mother, why was she at your flat? I need to know everything, Kate, if I'm going to help you."

"It was about the letters," I informed her.

"Letters?" Molly affirmed. "What letters?"

"The poisoned pen letters which have been

circulating the village."

"I see. Did you or your mother receive one of these letters?" she enquired as she scribbled hard in her notebook.

"I haven't, but mother said she had." I hoped her next question was not going to be about what was in the letter; as much as I disliked my mother I did not want to get her into trouble – fortunately it was not.

"Do you know if the police are aware of these letters?" she queried.

"Not as far as I know … I had been asked by the villagers to speak to my boyfriend about them, he's a police officer you see … Oh my god, James, we were supposed to be having dinner tonight, how could I have forgotten about James?" I whimpered, starting to fret.

"Don't worry, take a few deep breaths," Molly soothed, whilst pouring me out a glass of water. "I'll get a message to him straight away." She asked me to write down his number and a note on a piece of paper, which she passed onto the officer standing guard by the door. "Now let's go back to that phone call, was the message left on your answering machine?"

"Yes. I talked to him before he rang off to tell him what time I would be there, but yes, it was definitely left on my machine. Could that be helpful?"

"I'm not sure yet, but I can't emphasise enough that you have to remember every little detail." We seemed to talk for hours – it was getting late.

"Right, you missed the bus and had to walk. What time do you think you got to Lime House?"

"I think it was about six-thirty p.m.," I said, "the door was open so I went in."

"The door was open ... did you see anyone?" she asked.

I lowered my voice. "Yes, the spirit of Doctor Daniels appeared to me, he showed me where his body was lying." Molly sat back abruptly in her chair, before leaning in towards me.

"Well, I don't think it would be a good idea to bring that bit of information to the attention of the police," she whispered, looking round at the officer in the room, "but, off the record, did he say anything?"

"No, not a word, I kept talking to him but ..."

"Shame, he might have told you who killed him," she quipped, breaking briefly the sombre mood of the proceedings. "Ok. Let's go over everything again from the beginning. Did you see anyone when you were walking along the road, anyone at all?"

It took me a while to think; I was so tired, tired of going over the events repeatedly.

"Yes, yes." I suddenly remembered how could I have forgotten? "He almost knocked me over, Kevin ... Kevin Brown, one of our postmen, he saw me!"

An hour later, Molly finally called a halt to our conversation. "I think I have a few leads to work on. I'll get the police to listen to your answer machine and suggest they speak to Kevin Brown, and I'll have to tell them about the letters." She smiled a caring smile before continuing, "I'm afraid, Kate, you'll have to stay here tonight, but be assured I'll be back first thing in the morning. Keep positive." We both rose to our feet and once again she hugged me, before turning to leave.

I was immediately escorted back to my four grey walls, where I laid down reluctantly on the hard surface – my bed for the night. Slowly I drifted into a light sleep, interrupted occasionally by the wailing sounds of my fellow inmates. In my dream state, I found myself back on the village green. The spirit, I knew now as Sarah, took my hand and guided me back to Lime House. She told me to look at the scene in front of me with new eyes. I saw myself entering the library and then the appearance of Mrs. Norton brought to the fore exactly what I had missed.

CHAPTER 21 – THE INNOCENT AND THE GUILTY

I woke early the next morning and began pacing my cell, itching to get on with the task in hand. The dream I had just experienced had opened my eyes to new revelations about the events of the previous day – I desperately needed to talk to Molly. She was as good as her word and, after I had demolished the last morsel of toast and swigged the remaining drop of weak tea my captors had brought me, my cell door was thankfully unlocked once again, before I was transferred to an interview room, where Molly was patiently waiting. Unfortunately, we only had a few minutes to speak before two detectives, who introduced themselves as Chief Inspector Wheeler and Detective Sergeant Peters, joined us.

In addition to the glasses and water jug, a recording device now reposed on the side of the table.

"Right, Miss Oliver, I have to let you know this interview will be recorded and if necessary played in court, do you understand?" Chief Inspector Wheeler, who was leading the investigation, pointed out.

"Yes, I understand," I mumbled.

"I would ask you to answer my questions with a clear voice, please," the detective requested, before continuing, "I'm now starting the recording. Present is Chief Inspector Wheeler and Detective Sergeant Peters, together with Miss Kate Oliver and her barrister, Ms Brightman, is this correct?"

"Yes that's correct," I replied before he continued.

"Miss Oliver, yesterday, Friday seventh August 2009, at six-thirty p.m., you were discovered by Mrs. Norton, Doctor Daniels' housekeeper in the property known as Lime House, standing over the body of Doctor Michael Daniels, is this correct?"

"Not standing, I was sitting on the floor," I pointed out.

"Thank you for correcting me. I understand that last night you had a chance to speak to your barrister, Ms Brightman, and some new information you gave her has since been passed on to us, which I would like to add at this point has been very useful. In addition, the forensic team have had time to survey the crime scene and determine the cause of Doctor Daniels' death. Now, Miss Oliver, I need you to tell me in your own words what exactly happened yesterday."

I began as Molly had instructed me, from the morning events, but when I came to the part where Mrs Norton found me – I had new disclosures to make. I glanced at Molly to reassure her I knew what I was saying.

"I realised a few things last night ..." I began, recalling my dream. "I only set eyes on Doctor Daniels' body when I rounded the desk. It was impossible to see him from the door because his desk has a modesty board in front of it. So my question to you is," I was in full flow now, my confidence rising, "why did Mrs. Norton start screaming from the doorway, calling me a murderer, unless of course she already knew the doctor was lying there dead?" The detectives glanced quickly at each other, but I had not finished. "Also she said she had called the police; how would she have done that when she supposedly had only just discovered his body?" I sat back in the chair and Molly put her hand on my arm and squeezed it gently.

"Get it checked out, Peters. I'm going to stop the recording, Miss Oliver." At this point, the chief inspector also rose, and excused himself from the room.

"Well done, Kate," Molly enthused. "I haven't had a chance to tell you yet, but the police brought in Kevin Brown this morning, I think they're interviewing him right now."

The following minutes seemed like hours, before both detectives re-entered the room.

"Miss Oliver, I'm pleased to say for now you're free to go; your observations were correct and you can also thank your postman colleague for his evidence. Please see the custody officer on your way out."

I looked to the heavens and said a quiet thank you, before Molly and I sprang to our feet and embraced each other.

Back at the front desk, I had even more forms to sign. While Molly and I waited, we witnessed Mrs Norton being hauled off towards the cells in handcuffs, shouting at the top of her lungs that a man with a beard had framed her – and I knew this whole affair was far from over.

Entering the reception area, I was unexpectedly lifted off my feet by an over-enthusiastic Ben and father, who had apparently been waiting around in the station all night. Linking arms, the four of us headed out together into the car park, from where I noticed Kevin Brown getting into his car. Running over to him, I smiled broadly.

"Kevin, thanks for coming in, I hear you had something to do with my release."

"It was nothing, just told them how it was." He grinned.

"And how was that?" I asked.

"Well after I saw you, I drove around the next bend and came across that housekeeper of Doctor Daniels standing at the side of the road on her phone. Apparently, when they checked the time of the call she had made to the station, and the time you arrived at the house, well it didn't ... correlate or something," he dropped his voice, his face was now almost touching mine. "I also overheard something ... the police think Doctor Daniels was the poisoned pen writer."

"No!" I exclaimed. "I don't buy that, not Doctor Daniels."

"It makes sense when you think about it: people would confide in him, why even I told him ..." but he managed to stop himself from going any further. I thanked him once again and gave him a quick peck on his cheek, which seemed to put a spring in his step.

Father drove Molly to the train station and, as we said our goodbyes, I quietly promised I would let her know about our next 'Book Club' meeting.

"Right, young lady, you're coming to stay at the farm for a few days," father announced before I could interject. "Ronny has got your old room ready for you so I don't want any arguments, ok?" Then for the first time in years, he put his arm around me and kissed me gently on my forehead. Quite honestly, I was not going to argue; exhaustion had finally overtaken me, I sat back in his Land Rover and, with Ben at my side, closed my eyes.

***

"I've run you a bath and there are clean clothes on your bed," Ronny chirped as she greeted us at the farm house door, "the phone's been ringing nonstop, everyone is relieved you're home, no one believed for one minute ..."

"Thanks Ronny," I sighed, a bath was exactly what I needed to wash away the lingering stench of murder. Wearily, I climbed the stairs to the bathroom and peeled off my borrowed prison clothes. Lying back in the warm water, I rejoiced as the cleansing liquid enveloped my aching body. I began to contemplate the last twenty-four hours. Why, if it were true, would Mrs. Norton have killed Doctor Daniels? Moreover, why would the police suspect that he had been the poisoned pen letter writer? Perhaps Mrs. Norton had been a recipient of a letter herself, causing her such anguish that she had lost it with him. All this was pure conjecture of course, for now I just wanted to mourn the loss of a very fine gentleman.

"Are you decent?"

The face of my best friend appearing around my bedroom door unpredictably launched me into floods of tears. At length, with the help of Beth's soothing and comforting words, my sore and bloodshot eyes dried.

"Everyone's devastated over Doctor Daniels' death, so much so that I've cancelled the reunion, for the time being anyway," Beth declared delicately.

To be honest, this news was quite a relief, although I knew that deep down Beth was disappointed after all her hard work. We sat on my bed talking for some time, just as we used to, until Ronny's voice rose from the bottom of the stairs to inform us that dinner was ready.

The unexpected appearance of James at the farm brought me even more comfort and as I fell into his strong arms, he kissed me ardently on my lips. Inviting him into the house, I had no hesitation but to introduce him to everyone as my boyfriend. Quickly, Ronny found another plate and chair and as he settled down between Beth and me, Ben gave me a nudge and a wink.

"You're a dark horse, sis, and for the record, I approve."

With the meal completed, father suggested I showed James around the orchards. Our stroll brought back memories of Josh and me, but I knew I had to put those thoughts completely out of my mind, for those days were long gone, the future, whether it was with James or not, lay in front of me. He took my hand in his as we meandered along the lanes, heading in the direction of the meadow where I had lost my virginity, I explained it was my favourite place and as we climbed over the stile, James lifted me with ease to the ground before kissing me passionately.

Up to this point, we had not discussed Doctor Daniels' murder, however, now we were so far from the house and there was no one to overhear us, James brought up the subject.

"I can't tell you how distraught I was when I heard you'd been arrested; I knew of course you couldn't have killed him. I was desperate to come to the station but they wouldn't let me off duty, short staffed you see, and when I did manage to get away you had already been released," he conveyed apologetically before continuing. "They think they have evidence to convict Mrs. Norton," he related solemnly, "they believe the doctor was the writer of the poisoned pen letters, because apparently they found a letter addressed to her in the rubbish outside, accusing her of stealing from him. They've put two and two together and think she found out he had sent it and killed him before he told anyone else."

So, my suspicions were correct; obviously I was in the wrong profession. I explained I was still not convinced about the whole scenario and enlightened him about the cries Mrs. Norton had uttered when she was being taken down to the cells – haunting cries about a man with a beard, which kept reverberating around my head.

That night, as I lay in my old bed with all the familiar sounds around me, I thought of James once more and how I could not wait to be alone in my flat with him again; to hold him, to touch him and to feel his warm love within me ...

Waking the next morning, it took me a few minutes to comprehend where I was. It was a bit strange being back home, for although the decor had not changed much, the running of the house certainly had, notably with the absence of Flo, who now only worked two days a week. The rest of my stay gave me a chance to get to know Ronny a bit more, and I soon began to understand why father seemed to have fallen for her, as she was totally opposite to mother. For one thing, she was an excellent cook. However, by the time Tuesday arrived, I felt more than ready to return to my little flat.

***

A welcoming committee of villagers, including Flo, had accumulated in the post office, led by Barbara Hamilton.

"Kate, dear, we're so pleased to see you, it must have been a horrible ordeal for you, if there is anything any one of us can do, or if you just want to talk... you only have to ask." I thanked them all for their support and made my excuses.

"Yes, Kate needs some space," chirped Laura from behind the counter, "come through my dear, I've put some provisions in your fridge, so you can make yourself a nice cup of tea." Good old Laura, her answer to everything was a nice cup of tea. "I want you to take some time off," she added quietly. "Emily has agreed to help me in the shop, so you don't have to worry about anything," without pausing for breath, she continued, "by the way, the police searched your flat on Friday night and took your phone away, brought it back the next day though. I've since tidied up for you so you can't even tell they've been in." I hugged and thanked her before closing the door.

Home at last. I looked around, relieved to be back, because just for a brief moment, I had questioned if I would ever see my little sanctuary again. There it was, my little red dress still hanging on its hanger, sadly now redundant – no longer required. I opened my wardrobe door and placed it on the rail alongside my other garments. Almost at once, my eyes alighted on my little white jewellery box, hidden as if in disgrace, at the bottom of my wardrobe. Why was I still hiding my gift from Gabrielle after all these years, why was I so afraid to expose its presence? The time had come to put it in a pride of place on my dressing table for the whole world to see, for I was not a child anymore, no one could take it away from me now.

I was just beginning to relax when Beth turned up at my door, all fired up with excitement.

"Just spoken to Emma, she sends her love by the way. To put it briefly, it's all arranged, we're going to France tomorrow: you, Ben and me. Ronny said she'd look after Christopher. So, what do you think?"

What did I think? I thought it was a fantastic idea.

Later that afternoon, James arrived with a Chinese takeaway and a bottle of white wine, which we ate and drank with relish. When I told him I was going away for a few days, he reacted by lifting me up in his arms and carrying me into my bedroom.

"Well, we'd better make the most of the time we have together," he enthused, while he began to remove my clothes, exposing my naked form. How I had yearned for this moment, as his hands and mouth caressed the innermost parts of my body, stimulating my very being, I lay back as complete ecstasy overwhelmed me. He was truly a perfect lover.

The following morning, with my bags packed, we said our temporary goodbyes. I promised to call him as soon as we reached our destination, which was going be the French abode of Beth's grandparents. Driving out of the village, I thought of my childhood gift sitting on my dressing table, waiting in anticipation of my return, with an answer to the question that had haunted me for the best part of my life: the whereabouts of the woman who had presented it to me all those years ago.

CHAPTER 22 – DISCOVERIES

With great precision, Ben drove his new Range Rover up the ramp and into the parking area that lay within the bowels of the ship for the commencement of our ferry journey, which would take a couple of hours across the choppy sea, before docking at the French port of Calais.

Almost at once, the vessel began to sway and heave in the swell of the English Channel and I realised I was not as good a sailor as I had imagined I would be. Consequently, I had no other option but to spend most of the journey above deck to allow the sea breeze to alleviate my nausea. Both Ben and Beth were quick to join me.

"Did you know mother came round to see me on the morning of Doctor Daniels death?" I asked my brother as the three of us huddled together for warmth against the bracing air.

"No, but Flo said she had seen her in the village and that she and Jack were staying in the pub, so I went round there on that Friday evening to let her know what had happened to you, but apparently they had already packed up and left."

"Strange, she told me she was staying around for a few days. Apparently, she received one of those letters from the poisoned pen writer, she said accusing her of not paying her taxes, but I didn't believe her story."

Ben looked at me and then looked away. "Now

why doesn't that surprise me? You and mum – I have never really understood why you don't get on." Darling Ben, mother's golden child, he truly seemed oblivious to the way I had been treated in our early years.

With some relief, the sight of the French coast came into view. I found myself pondering over why mother had left so abruptly; had she found out who had written the letters and had her curiosity been satisfied, I wondered.

Stepping for the first time onto French soil brought me sheer delight; driving on the opposite side of the road, however, did not. It took Ben some time and a few near misses to become accustomed to this new way of driving, but eventually, more with luck than anything else, the three of us, and the Range Rover, arrived intact at the holiday home of Beth's grandparents.

The building sat in a breath-taking setting adjacent to a still, blue, shimmering lake on the outskirts of the town of Ardres. Impatient to show us around, Beth led us proudly from room to room, excited to be back in the house that held so many happy family memories for her. Before we had time to unpack, however, a knock at the door brought even more excitement in the form of Emma and her husband, Henri, who greeted us in the true French manner, with a kiss on both cheeks, before inviting us all to join them for dinner at a local restaurant.

Following a wonderful meal, which fortunately did not include either snails or frogs legs, we all came back to the house by the lake for coffee. Standing with Emma in the kitchen, thoroughly enjoying the aroma that was now wafting in my direction from the percolating coffee pot, she brought up the subject I had come all this way to discuss.

"Kate, would you like to come to my house tomorrow to talk about what I have found out about Gabrielle?"

"You can't tell me anything now?" I asked, trying to understand why we had to delay the discussion.

"I'd rather wait until tomorrow."

***

Next morning, we got up early to drive the short distance to Ardres and to the grey stone house of Emma and Henri, which nestled within a prime location, along a narrow street, five minutes' walk from the centre of the town. Henri had already left for his work at the bank, but Emma, fortunately, had managed to take a few days off from her job at the local tourist office.

She greeted us warmly and led us straight into her kitchen, where she had prepared a sumptuous breakfast, including the most delicious croissants I had ever tasted. Once we had finished and cleared the table, Emma produced a number of copies of old newspapers, which she painstakingly laid out in front of us.

"Ok, what are we looking at?" I began, trying to bring to mind some of the French I had learnt at school.

"Right ... I told you at Beth's wedding I recognised the name Gabrielle from somewhere, but it took me a while to recall where I had seen it. In fact, it had been on an old poster in the window of a baker's shop in a village a couple of miles away, but I still could not recollect what the poster had actually said. So, I decided to delve into the archives of the region's newspapers and came up with these articles, dating back some twenty years, concerning the disappearance of a Gabrielle Duval."

I was beside myself. "The disappearance of Gabrielle Duval, I ... don't understand, it's a different name!"

My mind was in a whirl, had I waited all this time to find out that, in fact, Emma was mistaken; had she unwittingly lifted my hopes only to dash them again? Fortunately, she had not yet finished with her investigative results as she carefully picked up another report, and pointed to a picture of a smiling Gabrielle Duval – or, as Ben and I knew her – Gabrielle Bayne. Choking back the tears at seeing the face of Gabrielle after so many years, I managed to pose the question, "What does it say below the picture?"

"I'll do my best to translate; this bit of the article is why I believed she was your Gabrielle. It says she had gone to England to live on a farm with a family as an au pair and that her mother had received a letter from her saying she had left the family and had decided to travel around England."

"I suppose that's possible, isn't it?" joined in Ben, "I mean, I was too young to know what was happening at the time, but from what you told me, sis, she left under a bit of a cloud, perhaps she was too ashamed to go home."

I was not convinced. I had loved Gabrielle and I knew she had loved me and even after all this time, I did not believe she was a thief, even though now it seemed she was not as honest a person as I had thought she was.

"This other article," Emma went on, picking up yet another broadsheet, "relates to an interview with Gabrielle's mother, who opens up about her family's other tragic loss two years earlier: the death of her oldest daughter, Alita."

"Poor woman!" exclaimed Beth, "the loss of a child is unbearable in itself but to lose two in as many years; she must have felt like her whole world was collapsing around her."

"We still don't know if Gabrielle ever came back, I mean these stories are old," I pointed out, trying to keep positive about the whole thing.

"Yes, I agree," responded Emma. "That's why I have been trying to find Madame Duval." She reached into her pocket and produced a piece of paper. "She was a very difficult lady to trace, simply because she had remarried and moved away, but just last week I got lucky." Emma handed me the paper with the name of a Madame Cecilia Reiner, together with her telephone number. "Do you want me to call her and ask if we can visit? Looking at the post code, it's only a couple of hours drive from here."

We all agreed it was the best idea, so while Emma spoke sensitively to Gabrielle's mother, Madame Reiner, on the phone in impeccable French, we waited with bated breath for the outcome.

"Ok, she'll see us. I didn't go into too much detail, but she knows you are from England and knew Gabrielle," Emma turned to me and took my hand in hers. "She is still missing ... I'm so sorry."

Deep down, I had felt there was not much hope ... but now, at least, I had the chance to meet her mother and learn a bit more about her and her sister.

Indeed, it only took two hours to drive south

towards the town of Montreuil, mercifully this time with a confident Emma at the wheel. A well-dressed thirty-something woman, who introduced herself as the cleaner, greeted us at the door of the three-story home, before showing us into an elegant room adorned with antique furniture. Reclining in a high backed velvet chair positioned next to a window overlooking the street outside, was Madame Cecilia Reiner.

She was a woman about sixty years old and of small stature, well dressed in a simple black suit, and around her neck hung a single strand of pearls. Her pleasant features lit up at once when she saw us walk into the room, and immediately she beckoned us to join her at her place of vigil. Frustratingly, she spoke very little English and as neither Ben nor I could converse confidently in French, we had no option but to communicate with her through Emma.

Overcome with joy at finding out that we were the children Gabrielle had been looking after in England, she cried and hugged us as if we were her own. Ben found this open outpouring of emotion from a stranger a bit unnerving, but I found it strangely comforting. Cecilia, for that is how she asked us to call her, divulged that Gabrielle would write often about her life with us. She spoke at great length, and with immense sadness, at the despair she felt about not knowing what had happened to her beautiful daughter.

Apparently, the French police tried for years to locate Gabrielle, but there were very few leads to work on, and eventually the family had no option but to give up any hope of her ever being found alive. While Emma translated her story, I realised Cecilia seemed to be studying me carefully – had Gabrielle disclosed how close we had been, had she revealed she had given me her sister's jewellery box?

Our time with Cecilia ended all too soon and I was very much aware we had not asked about her oldest daughter, but perhaps that was none of our business. Standing to leave, I noticed for the first time an ornate oval framed picture of two dark haired little girls dressed in their Sunday best.

I stopped, mesmerised for a moment, in front of this moving sight of Gabrielle and Alita, before turning back to ask for confirmation from Cecilia, that these were her daughters – however, she had already turned away and was focusing once again on the window, seemingly unaware of our imminent departure. The cleaner, who also appeared to be about to leave, showed us to the front door.

"Thank you," I said without thinking.

"You're welcome," she replied.

"You speak English," commented Ben, surprised.

"Yes, a little, I also work for an English couple, the lady has been teaching me. My name is Elise, pleased to meet you." Elise shook us each by the hand – obviously, she had also learnt about British traditions as well.

"Elise, we are going for a coffee, do you have time to join us?" I asked, eager for the chance to find out more about the Duval family.

"Yes, I would very much like that," she replied. Two streets away from the Reiner's home, we came across a family-run café and, as is the custom in these parts, sat outside with the locals, making the most of the warm weather. It was immediately obvious that Elise was delighted to be in a position to practice her

English, with her tales of intrigue concerning her employers.

Apparently, she had worked for Monsieur and Madame Reiner ever since they married and moved to Montreuil, almost twelve years ago. Madame Reiner, she found, kept herself to herself and hardly had any visitors, consequently, mainly out of loneliness, she would often confide in Elise her innermost thoughts.

"Do you know anything about Alita, her oldest daughter?" I asked as I added yet another spoonful of sugar into my incredibly strong coffee.

"It was so sad, it happened long before I met Madame, of course," Elise began, "the poor girl hung herself from a tree in woods not far from Ardres." The four of us gasped in disbelief at the thought of anyone so young, being so desperate to kill themselves in that fashion.

"Did they … know why she did it?" Ben asked, trying to be diplomatic.

"I don't believe so, at least Madame never told me. They buried her in a cemetery several kilometres from Ardres; I can find out where if you wanted to visit her grave."

"Yes, thank you Elise," I responded quietly before continuing. "Do you know what happened to her father?"

"Monsieur Duval, they say, died of a broken heart after Gabrielle disappeared. Obviously it was too much for the poor man to bear."

We all fell silent for a while, trying to digest the awful tragedy that had befallen the family. No wonder Cecilia seemed slightly detached from reality; the unfortunate woman had been through an appalling ordeal.

"What about Monsieur Reiner, do you see much of him?" Emma enquired. Elise began to blush slightly before brushing her dark hair seductively from her face.

"Joseph … Reiner is a businessman; he's away a lot …"

I could not help but realise that Elise had used his Christian name; was there more to their relationship than employee and employer, I contemplated. Were they, in fact, lovers? This was France after all, where, if the films I had watched were to be believed, romance was everywhere. On top of this, Elise was definitely dressed a little too well to be just a cleaner.

"He is younger than Madame," she continued, without being prompted, "some people say he married her for her money, but I don't think he would have been so cruel … he's kind to me anyway."

She picked up her coffee cup and sipped slowly at its contents. Yes, I thought, she is having an affair with Monsieur Joseph Reiner.

Realising we had leapt into somewhat intimate territory, Beth quickly changed the subject. "Madame Reiner said she had received letters from Gabrielle, did she ever show them to you, Elise?"

"Why yes, she reads them all the time, Gabrielle had very nice handwriting. It struck me as strange though, that the last letter she received from her, saying she was going to travel around England … had been typed on a typewriter and not handwritten.

"Yes," I cut in, "that was strange and if Gabrielle had already left our house, why and where would she have had the opportunity to use a typewriter?" Now I had even more unanswered questions to consider.

"I'm sorry, I must go; I'll be late for … my appointment." Elise got to her feet with the intention of leaving.

"Before you go, Elise, can you tell me why Madame Reiner sits staring out of the window?"

Elise smiled. "She is simply waiting for Gabrielle to return."

The pain in my chest hardened as further emotion mounted in me.

"Here, take this, it's my telephone number, Elise," indicated Emma, producing a business card from her handbag, "please phone if you find out about the place where Alita is buried and please pass this number to Madame Reiner, just in case she wants to talk to us anymore."

With Elise turning once again to leave, my imagination went into overdrive. Did she have a rendezvous with Monsieur Reiner in some sordid hotel? I hoped I was wrong because I quite liked her.

We arrived back at the house by the lake just as it was getting dark and almost immediately, as Beth turned the key in the lock, the phone began to ring. It was Elise, with directions to Alita's grave.

The following day, we set off on a macabre outing, to say the least, but something I just felt we had to do. After some stressful map reading, we arrived at a small village church, the gravestones surrounding it neglected to the point of abandonment – not surprisingly therefore, the whole place evoked an eerie atmosphere.

"Beth, if you and Emma take the right hand side, Kate and I can take the left," instructed Ben, trying to organise us in the daunting task of locating Alita, as quickly as possible, amongst the hordes of graves that lay in front of us.

Half an hour later a cry, which erupted from Beth, that she had found it, had us all rushing to her side. However, before I reached the place where Beth and the others were now standing, a very strange feeling came over me. Then I saw her – my spirit friend, who had not appeared to me for years – but here she was, after all this time in front of me and to my surprise, a smile radiated from her. She glided silently alongside me until I reached the others, who were oblivious to her presence.

"Are you ok, Kate?" inquired Beth, looking at me with compassion as she took hold of my hand, believing I was feeling emotional in the wake of finding Gabrielle's sister.

"Yes …" I replied softly.

Attempting to decipher the inscription on the moss-covered gravestone, a feeling of immense sadness flooded over me. Alita Duval was only nineteen years old when she took her own life – what a dreadful waste.

I bent down and tried, with the help of the others, to tidy the area as best as I could, pulling hard at the long grasses and nettles which were trying to disguise the fact that a sweet, troubled girl lay beneath its soil. With the task completed, I stood up and looked around, realising instantly that my spirit friend had left me, once again. Why had she appeared in the first place, and why here, in France?

Three days later, we left the French shores behind us. I swore to myself, as the ferry began its journey home, that I would return some day, because I believed there was still so much more to Gabrielle's life I needed to know about.

CHAPTER 23 – A FUNERAL

Over a week had now passed since we returned home from France, but I still could not get the images of Gabrielle and her family out of my head.

"Kate, I said ten second-class stamps, not ten first-class stamps," pointed out Pat Wood as she stood patiently at the head of the queue of customers, which had been building up all morning.

"So sorry, Pat, my mind's elsewhere," I apologised as I quickly rectified my mistake.

"Yes it must be, my dear, it's the funeral tomorrow, isn't it? Such an awful business, I think there will be a good turnout though, everyone's talking about it." I nodded. "I mean," she continued, "even if he was the poisoned pen writer as they say he was, he was still a good doctor none the less."

I felt incredibly incensed. "The speculation that he wrote those damn letters is still hearsay as far as I am aware and, as the law states, a man is innocent until proven guilty, and as the poor man is no longer with us to defend himself, I don't want to hear any more bad words said about him!" My outburst brought a sudden silence, followed by a low muttering.

"Kate, my dear," coaxed Laura, emerging from the back room, "why don't you go and have an early extended lunch; I can cope here."

Finding myself unexpectedly outside on a chilly autumn day, I took my sandwich and set out on a stroll to try to clear my thoughts – not entirely sure of my destination, I headed out towards the village green. The face of Doctor Daniels lying so cold in his own blood came once again to the fore. I knew now, from James, that he had died from suffocation following a massive blow to the head, but I was still not convinced that Mrs. Norton was the killer, although surprisingly it seemed I was the only one to question her guilt. Her rages about a man with a beard had had me trying to recall all the males in the district with facial hair. Most men I knew were clean-shaven, the exception being the Reverend Stanton, whose goatee had always given him a look of distinction, I thought, but not one of a potential killer and anyway, Mrs. Norton would have recognised him immediately.

Arriving at the duck pond on the edge of the green, I sat down on the wooden bench, and began tossing my crusts into the deep, murky waters, while watching with pleasure as a mother duck and her three ducklings fought over the small morsels.

"So this is what you get up to during the day; I thought you had a full time job?" Beth mocked as she and Christopher joined me.

"Extended lunch hour, things are getting on top of me slightly," I confessed to my friend, "just been thinking about Doctor Daniels. The day he died … Beth, I saw his spirit … it led me to his body." This disclosure, of yet another manifestation, obviously troubled her.

"Kate, don't you think it's time you told Ben and your dad about … well … about the fact you can communicate with the dead?" She spoke softly, covering Christopher's ears as she did so, just in case the infant understood what she was saying. "Part of you must want to tell them and to be honest I don't quite understand how you've managed to keep it from them all these years. When we were in France and you told me your spirit friend had been with us ... well I mean ... aren't you afraid when they materialize in front of you like that? I know I would be terrified."

"No, I'm never afraid; their appearances have always been for a reason, usually to tell me something or to give me comfort, but never with evil intentions." I was thoughtful for a brief moment. "Maybe you're right; maybe it's time to tell Ben and father." I headed back to the shop, realising my revelation to my family might mean they would see me in a different light in the future, but at least for the first time, they will know exactly who I am.

***

James met me at the outside steps of my flat after work.

"Do you fancy going anywhere special tonight?" he asked as he helped me up with my shopping.

"Why, it's not your birthday or anything is it?" I replied curiously.

"No it's not my birthday; however it is an anniversary of sorts." He spun me round and kissed me affectionately. "We've been together two months today, just thought we should celebrate something good after so much sadness, that's all."

"It's a lovely idea, but I'm not really in the mood, been a bad day, I just want to relax at home ... sorry." I reached into my shopping bag and pulled out a bottle of wine and two rump steaks. "How do you fancy Steak Diane and a bottle of Merlot?"

"I'll tell you what, you go and run yourself a nice bath and I'll prepare dinner." How could I say no, especially as James had yet to show me his culinary skills?

Sometime later, I lay back in the soothing waters I had filled with exotic oils, enjoying the intoxicating aroma being expelled in the vapours around me. Slowly, the door of the bathroom opened and James entered carrying a large glass of wine.

"I thought you might like a drink to add to your self-indulgence." He grinned, positioning the glass down on the side of the bath, a look of desire growing in his eyes. "Would you like me to wash your back?"

"Just my back?" I teased as he knelt down and began cleansing my shoulders and arms. Slowly, he moved his hands to my more intimate places, causing me to groan with the sheer pleasure his caresses were bringing me. "Oh James," I cried, "make love to me."

Carefully, he reached down and lifted me from the waters, drenching his clothes with his romantic gesture, before carrying me into the bedroom and placing me gently on my bed. His sodden garments fell to the floor before we came together with such passion that I thought I would explode with the sheer intensity of it all.

We eventually ate our dinner, some two hours later – it was the best steak I had ever tasted.

The next morning my mood had changed dramatically, for it was the moment I had been dreading. Once I had zipped up my little black dress and slipped on my kitten heels, I searched around for the handbag I had not used since that fateful day. When I finally located it at the top of my wardrobe, I inserted a packet of tissues I thought I might need later. Then my eyes alighted on the envelope I had completely forgotten about, the one I had removed from the doctor's house with my name on it. Perhaps now was not the appropriate time to view its contents, instead, I decided to store it in the top drawer of my dressing table to open later.

***

At eleven o'clock, the slow deep sound of the church bells began reverberating around the village, calling us all to the funeral of a much-admired man. Shops closed their doors as mourners from Willow Green and the surrounding villages attended the funeral of Doctor Daniels.

The ancient pews were quickly full to capacity, so many had no other option but to stand outside in the grounds of the churchyard and listen to this unprecedented event from the loud speakers, which had been especially erected for the occasion. Laura and I managed to get seats inside the church, together with Brenda and Flo, who squeezed my hand warmly as we settled down to wait for the proceedings to commence. Looking around me, I could see several familiar faces, including the detectives involved in investigating the doctor's death, who happened to be sitting next to Charles and Barbara Hamilton, however, to my relief, the elusive Stephen was nowhere to be seen.

The Reverend Stanton took his place in the pulpit as the doors of the church creaked open and the sunlight flooded in through the arched entrance. Slowly, the coffin began its solemn journey up the aisle, supported by six pallbearers, who included Ben and father. As the coffin was gently placed in front of the altar, the voices of the congregation rang out in homage. This was followed by an emotional eulogy from the Reverend who, like a good number of us, had known the doctor most of his life. Lastly, rising reluctantly to their feet, were two strangers to the village, Jeremy and Graham Daniels, who went on to give a moving tribute to their father, which they just about managed to complete before breaking down in tears. Overall, it was a perfect funeral, for a perfect man.

With the event over, the church gradually emptied and the throngs of people began to disperse. I told Laura I would be along in a minute as I was hoping to grab a chance to speak with Jeremy and Graham before they left, fortunately, I did not have long to wait. Accompanied by the Reverend and Emily Stanton, the brothers soon appeared down the church steps.

"So sorry about your father, he was a wonderful man," I began as I stepped forward, interrupting their conversation. "My name is Kate Oliver; I was the one who found your father's body." The brothers seemed rather taken aback by my boldness in approaching them and looked as if they were unsure how to react to me, so I continued. "I was at the house because Doctor Daniels wanted to give me some old pictures from his time at Willow Green Primary, I have them at my flat, I'm sure you'd like them back ... I could drop them off at Lime House, if that's where you're staying?"

"Actually, we're staying at the pub, the police want a bit longer to carry out their investigations," the shorter of the two men replied, holding out his hand to shake mine. "I'm Graham, by the way, I understand you were a big help to the police in finding our father's killer."

"Let's just say I proved I didn't do it; as to Mrs. Norton's guilt, that's for the law to decide."

"Interesting," interjected Jeremy thoughtfully, "anyway, we are staying for her trial, which we've been told will be in a month's time and in any case we have so much to sort out ... so there's no hurry for the pictures. It was nice to meet you, Kate Oliver, if you want to join us at the pub for a drink, you'd be most welcome." They both shook my hand before turning to walk away, seemingly with the intention of continuing their conversation with the Stantons.

I was not ready to go back to the post office quite yet – I just needed a bit longer to compose myself. Meandering amongst the well-maintained cemetery, a real contrast to where poor Alita's body lay, I wondered who was looking after the grounds now, since Harold, whose job it had been to keep everything neat and tidy, had become so ill. Nearing the end of the pathway, I happened to stumble across the grave of Ernest Reed, Emily's father.

"Fucking old fool of a soldier, deserved all he fucking got," I spun around in alarm to find standing behind me none other than Stephen Hamilton, completely out of his head on drink. Adding even more disrespect to his vile words, he began to pour the remaining beer from his almost empty can over Ernest's headstone.

"Go away Stephen, crawl back to where you've just come from," I seethed.

"Ooh ... little miss prissy wants me, come on you

know you do."

In horror, I realised he was beginning to undo his trousers and, as the garment descended to his ankles, he lost his footing, toppled over, and fell sprawling onto Ernest's grave. It was a comical scene and if he were not such a depraved character, and someone I despised to the full, I would have laughed aloud. As I watched him attempting to clamber back to his feet, like a fish out of water, I only wished I had a camera to record the antics of this low-life. Just at that moment, quite unexpectedly, a cool breeze began to circle around us and from nowhere in particular, someone not of this world whispered softly in my ear.

"He was Ernest's killer!"

Of course he was.

CHAPTER 24 - FEELINGS

"James, what would you say if I told you someone from the spirit world had given me the name of a killer?"

"Ok, you've got my attention, are we talking about Doctor Daniels?"

"No, Ernest Reed, Emily Stanton's father."

It was the evening after the funeral and James and I were snuggling up together in front of the television, whilst devouring a very large pepperoni pizza.

"I know it was a long time ago, but do you think the police would listen to me?"

"Oh darling," he had never called me darling before, "I do love you ..." and, oh my god, he definitely had not told me he loved me before, how should I react? Should I carry on with our discussion or should I ... well should I say it back to him? I decided to continue talking as if ... well, as if it was a slip of the tongue on his part.

"If you're going to say the police will think I'm mad, you're right of course, but I just can't ignore what I was told, can I?"

"They'll say they need evidence ... evidence from this world and, as you say, it was a long time ago and anyway you've not told me who it was yet."

"Stephen Hamilton."

"Stephen Hamilton? But he could only have been a teenager at the time."

"Yes, but apparently he showed definite signs of

evil from an early age, if the village gossips are to be believed." I went on to relate the altercation I had had with Stephen in the cemetery.

"Are you ok, did the bastard touch you?" James demanded. As he took me in his arms I smiled at the look of concern rapidly erupting on his face.

"No, he didn't touch me; he's just a pathetic worm, that's all." Obviously relieved at my answer, James slumped back into the settee.

"Stephen Hamilton, well, well, what I would do to see that scum behind bars, preferably with his trousers on. Look, when I go in tomorrow I will try and dig out all the old records on the case, can't promise anything, but I'll have a look to see if there had been any question about Ernest Reed's accident. In the meantime, Miss Oliver," he pulled me towards him, brushed my hair gently from my face, and looked adoringly into my eyes, "how about an early night?"

Next morning, after James had left, I began to deliberate the dilemmas now facing me over the two potential murders in our once idyllic village. I was confident James would do all he could to find out any information on Ernest, so I decided for the time being to concentrate my thoughts wholly on Doctor Daniels and try to prove Mrs. Norton innocent by exposing his actual killer. For I still strongly believed he or she was still out there somewhere, perhaps now overly confident they had got away with murder, and anyway, I felt I owed the doctor.

Although hesitant about stepping on the toes of the police, and being accused of meddling by the locals, I decided I just had to try to talk to Mrs. Norton at the prison, where the poor woman was being held on remand. So, before I went into work, I made a quick phone call to see if she would agree for me to visit her. The female official I spoke to promised she would ring me back later with an answer. At three-fifteen p.m., I finally received the confirmation I had been eagerly awaiting: Mrs. Norton had agreed to see me – we managed to arrange a mutually agreed time for the following Wednesday, my next half day. Meanwhile, I looked forward to James's return.

The appearance of Ben in the shop just before closing was a bit of a surprise; his proposal, in hindsight, was not.

"Hi sis, Beth asked me to pop in to ask you and James to dinner this Saturday, she's asked dad and Ronny too, so it will be a bit of a party, what do you think, are you up for it?" Dear Beth; I knew what this was about, confession time, my confession time.

"Yes I can come, but I can't promise James will be able to, I'll have to check with him. Tell Beth I'll text her tomorrow."

***

James was much later than usual, in fact I was beginning to think I had been stood up, until a soft knocking at my door revealed my handsome police officer, looking tired and drawn. Apparently, it had taken James hours to locate the files and then several more to sift through all the statements and doctor's reports.

"Did you read anything to indicate it wasn't an accident?" I asked, hoping for a positive response, as I handed him a cold lager.

"Not exactly, but there was an interesting statement from a garage mechanic, who said he had done a maintenance check on the bike only a couple of days before the incident and he really couldn't understand how the wheel had come off so easily. Unfortunately, his statement doesn't seem to have been taken into consideration when the coroner gave his verdict – not sure why. By the way, the doctor was Doctor Daniels; thought you might find that interesting."

"I suppose he must have given evidence for many unusual deaths in the village over the years. You look whacked by the way; it's late, how about staying the night and we can talk more tomorrow?" We lay holding each other in the dimming light, before James suddenly turned to face me.

"You never said anything when I told you I loved you last night. I do, you know." My heartbeat rose in my chest. I looked deep into his eyes and I knew; knew that this wonderful, sexy man lying next to me was also the kindest, most thoughtful person I had ever met – how could I not love him?

"James …" I began slowly, before he managed to interrupt me.

"Ok, perhaps it's too soon, if you don't feel the same, I understand … I do really. Forget I said anything …"

I rolled over and lay on top of him.

"James … I love you too." We didn't make love that night, we simply held each other until we both drifted off into the most peaceful sleep I had had for a very long time.

My text to Beth the following morning was short and to the point. *'Beth thanks for invite, James can make it, wondering if you had room for two more? Would like to ask Flo and Laura, thought might need some back up.'*

Beth's reply was even shorter. *'Yes, that's fine, dinner's at 7.'*

I knew father and Ben would need some convincing following my revelation to them about my psychic abilities and having Flo and Laura there to support me, two individuals whose opinions father especially would respect, brought me some reassurance of the success of my impending announcement.

***

"Sorry we're late," I apologised, as I handed Beth a large bunch of mixed flowers bought at the last minute from the petrol station. "Wow, the table looks great Beth; you've really gone to town."

Father and Ronny were already settled in the two cosy armchairs situated on either side of a roaring fire, which was sending out an intense heat encompassing the entire room. Holding a glass of red wine in his hand, father stood at once, albeit unsteadily, to greet us.

"Flo and Laura, how nice to see you, come and sit with us, it's definitely the warmest place in the cottage," invited father, although we hardly had time to get comfortable when Beth announced dinner was ready.

An hour later, the satisfyingly pleasing sound of the stacking of empty plates, a true complement to Beth's cooking, announced the end of our banquet. As Beth rose to clear the table, I followed her into her small country kitchen and offered to do the washing up.

"No," she whispered quietly, "go back in there and start a conversation about you know what ... I'll be in there in a minute. Go on ...!" she urged, pushing me towards the door.

"Here's my beautiful daughter ... Don't you think she's beautiful, James?" father declared as I re-entered the dining room.

"Jonathan, dear, I think you could do with a coffee," pointed out Ronny, obviously embarrassed at father's inebriated state.

"Are you saying I'm drunk, Ronny darling? No, I've had a drink, maybe two or three, but I'm not drunk, no, I'm definitely not drunk."

"Well that's good father," I suddenly piped up, "because there's something I wanted to tell you and Ben."

"You're not getting bloody married, are you? I mean, no offense James, but you hardly know one another."

I blushed profusely at father's embarrassing outburst.

"No father, I'm not getting married ... but I want to tell you something important, important to me anyway ... I'm a medium," I blurted out, causing a deadly hush to descend upon my assembled friends, just as Beth entered with a steaming pot of coffee.

"Coffee anyone?"

"You're a fucking what?" father roared, before turning towards Laura and Flo, who seemed to have been traumatised by the whole debacle. "So sorry ladies, please excuse my language. What did you say, Kate? You're a med ..."

"I'm a medium, father; I can communicate with

dead people." My confidence in my announcement was beginning to wane rapidly – intuitively, James took my hand in his.

"Don't be so bloody stupid ... Ben, did you hear what your sister has just said?" father growled.

"I am sitting right here, dad, I can hear. Kate, what sort of a joke is this? You're upsetting Laura and Flo."

Both women managed to find their voices at the same time. "No, we're not upset," they chorused in harmony, while Beth placed a large mug of coffee before father, who began to sip it eagerly.

"Do you know what Kate is talking about, Beth?" demanded Ben, who had now risen to his feet and was pacing up and down the room.

"Yes, as a matter of fact, I do, she has a great gift. You must both listen to her. Go on Kate, tell them ... tell them about 'The Ladies Book Club'."

For the following, what seemed like, hours, I related to my father, brother and Ronny my experiences with the spirit world. Everyone sat in silence apart from the occasional gasp, mostly from Ronny who seemed the most freaked out by my story. Coming to the end of my tale, I sat back exhausted in my chair – James was still holding my hand.

"So," father began, "everyone in the room knew about this power of yours, apart from me and your brother."

"And me," pointed out Ronny.

"Yes, and you," father retorted, rather aggravated.

"The time never seemed right," I began apologetically, "I thought you would laugh at me or think I was crazy."

Father rose from his chair and moved silently towards me, before crouching down by my side.

"What hurts most is you didn't trust me or Ben, but I'm glad you've told us now. I love you, you silly girl, and I'm proud of you. Goodness knows where you got this gift of yours from, I don't know of anyone on my side of the family with any psychic abilities." He leaned forward and kissed me softly. I looked over at Flo, who seemed relieved at not being held accountable for my early introduction into the world of mediumship. A deep discussion ensued about the afterlife; everyone seemed to have his or her own opinion, especially Ben, who was sceptical about the whole concept.

"Ok then, show us, show us these powers of yours," he finally erupted.

"Ben, how could you? Kate, you don't have to prove anything, the rest of us know," cried Beth, trying to soothe the situation.

Laura, who had been quite quiet all evening, at last found the conviction to voice her opinion. "The ambience has to be right and quite honestly, I'm feeling a lot of hostility from you, young man, just now. Your sister is a remarkable person, who has brought a lot of joy to a great many people."

"It's ok Laura, really. Ben, I will try to show you, but I can't promise anything, it's not like the movies you know; spirits are not going to just miraculously appear. Sometimes nothing happens at all, but yes, for you, I will try. Can we move to the sitting room Beth, perhaps take a few chairs through?"

It only took us a few minutes to sort out the arrangements required for our circle. I noticed Ronny was looking a little anxious, so I told her she could go home if she wanted to, but she insisted she was fine and wanted to stay.

After we were all seated, I asked everyone to bow their heads and try to clear their minds. The air around me cooled rapidly and, as my eyes closed, Sarah appeared to me once more. Without uttering a single word, she reached towards me, took my hand in hers, and led me gracefully into her world.

I had never met my paternal grandfather, although I had seen several pictures of him, but suddenly there he was in front of me, pointing towards the bottom of the stairs at the farmhouse. Father had told me Grandfather Tom had died as the result of a fall and that he had been distraught at finding his misshapen body in the hall. However, in the vision I was being shown, the presence of another figure hovering over him caused me some concern at first, until I realised it was a woman holding a pillow to rest the poor man's head. I took the opportunity to have a conversation with my grandfather, who told me he was completely content where he was – united again with his beloved wife, my grandmother.

Re-entering our world, I looked around at the faces now staring anxiously in my direction.

"Are you alright? We were all worried about you, you were having trouble breathing," father's voice sounded frantic.

I insisted I was in good health and unaware I had been fighting for breath. I conveyed to everyone my visit with my grandfather, a disclosure that moved father to tears. When I revealed I had witnessed a woman at the scene, however, he was more than a little taken aback.

"Don't know who that could have been, your mother was the only woman living in the house at the time and she was out shopping; she certainly didn't appear until after the ambulance arrived."

I was not going to get into an argument over such a small matter because, apart from Ben's outburst, it had been such a pleasant evening. Had I convinced Ben of my ability? I was not sure, he never really said, but at least I would be forever grateful to my best friend for persuading me to open up to my family, and thankful for a new feeling of closeness between my father and me.

CHAPTER 25 – A SAD TALE

Shuffling uncomfortably on the hard wooden seat, awaiting Mrs. Norton's appearance, I shuddered at the thought it could easily have been me incarcerated in this dingy excuse of a prison. Eventually, the door to the visitor's room opened and I stood to greet the woman who had accused me of committing the crime she was now being held for. Looking tired and drawn, Mrs. Norton showed no emotion on her pallid face – just, it appeared, acceptance of her situation.

"Well, I have to admit I couldn't believe it when I was told you wanted to see me; come to gloat have you?" she jeered.

"No," I replied honestly, "I want to help you."

"Help me? But I tried to frame you; you must hate me." Her disposition towards me immediately changed and her eyes began to mist over. "I did such a bad thing." She looked down at her hands squeezing them together tightly, pushing her nails deep into her skin, punishing herself for her misdemeanour. I rose at once to my feet, went over to her, and put my arm around her shoulders.

"Mrs. Norton, I don't believe you killed Doctor Daniels." She stared at me with her haunted hollow eyes, as I retook my place opposite her.

"You don't?"

"No, I don't. I heard you the day they brought you into the police station; you were shouting about a man with a beard, have you any idea who he was?"

Mrs. Norton gazed far out in front of her as if in a trance.

"No one believes there was such a man, not even my ruddy solicitor, they all think I killed the doctor, but I didn't, how could I? He was a wonderful and kind person. But I did such a bad thing," she repeated.

"What was the bad thing you did?" I asked gently, believing she meant accusing me of murder.

"I stole from him; I'm so ashamed. I stole things over a long period: silver, ornaments, mostly small things, it's such a big house – he never ever noticed they were missing. Then I got one of those poisoned pen letters accusing me of stealing. How would anyone have known, I ask you, how could anyone have known?" She looked at me, pleading for an answer, but I had none to offer.

"I see, so you stole from Doctor Daniels, but where does the man with the beard come into the story?" I listened intently as Mrs. Norton related the events of that fateful day.

"That Friday started like any other," she began, "I made the doctor's breakfast and afterwards he retreated into his study to tackle his correspondence and to make a few phone calls. Later, following a light lunch, he informed me he was expecting two visitors during the afternoon, one of them being you, Miss Oliver. So, when the doorbell rang at two-thirty, I was quite prepared to greet the doctor's first caller, although I have to admit, I was taken aback slightly by his weird appearance. It was a man wearing a beige raincoat, sunglasses and gloves; to be honest, what with the glasses and the beard, there was not much of his face visible to the naked eye. I showed him into the study and the doctor asked if I would go and post a letter for him, before bringing in afternoon tea for them both. I recall at the time thinking the doctor seemed a bit edgy, but I put that thought to the back of my mind as I later prepared the tray of refreshments."

Mrs. Norton took out a tissue and wiped her eyes.

"Sorry ... when I went back into the study, which was probably about three quarters of an hour later, Doctor Daniels was nowhere to be seen, but the stranger was busy rifling through his files as bold as brass, creating a shower of paper which was soaring in all directions. I protested, of course, quite verbally in fact, at the mess he was making, but the bastard simply ignored me. It was not until I walked behind the desk ... that I first saw the doctor lying battered on the ground ... please forgive me, I just need a moment," she whimpered.

"I'm sorry, it must be so difficult for you to have to go over all this again, please take your time," I insisted, trying to be supportive. After several minutes, the unfortunate woman had composed herself enough to continue.

"I began screaming hysterically, which stopped his annihilation of the files, but then he grabbed me from behind and placed his hand over my mouth to suppress my cries," she closed her eyes tightly, momentarily recalling the terror she felt. "He snarled that he would kill me too. I was so scared, so very scared. Then, he threatened that if I didn't co-operate, he would make it look as if I had killed the doctor. So, you see, I felt I had no choice. He said Doctor Daniels had told him he was expecting you about six o'clock and, if I played my cards right, I could make it look as if you had killed him. Between us, we hatched a plan to frame you and it would have worked, except for one thing, you missed the bus – it's almost a funny scenario, isn't it?" she concluded.

However, I was not laughing. I was angry. Why would a complete stranger want to frame me for murder? He could have so easily walked away. Mrs. Norton had not recognised him, so why try to pin the killing on me?

"Mrs. Norton, I can't say I'm not sick about what you tried to do to me, but I do believe your story and still want to help you, if I can. First, I know an eminent barrister, Molly Brightman. I could ask if she would take your case – can't promise anything, though. I mean, if you feel your current solicitor doesn't believe in you, I don't think you will stand much of a chance in court. Secondly, we definitely need to unearth that stranger; is there anything else you can remember about him that would help me to find him, anything at all?

"Believe me, I've gone over that afternoon again and again in my head, but I've got nothing to add, I really wish I did."

"Please think, can you remember anything more about his appearance even?" I implored her.

"Hmm … well, I suppose the colour of his beard was a little, let's say, startling, he had dark hair, but his beard was definitely ginger."

"Right, good, well that's something. Anything else? Please think, Mrs. Norton."

"Well … I did think it peculiar at the time that the study window was unlocked. The doctor hated sitting in a draught and there it was, wide open, with a strong breeze blowing through it."

Just at that moment, a prison guard informed us our time was up. Mrs. Norton looked at me directly. "Thank you, I know I don't deserve your support. Look, I've thought about what you said and I think you're right, I need a new brief, so please contact this Molly Brightman, if you think there's a chance she would be interested in defending me."

"Of course, I'll contact her as soon as I get home."

***

Arriving back at the village a few hours later, I really felt I needed to talk to someone; James was on night duty, so I decided to pay Flo a visit. As soon as Flo opened her front door, a nauseating odour of disinfectant and vomit saturated the air. Fortunately I managed to curb the urge to show my abhorrence of the aroma invading my nostrils. Flo greeted me warmly and invited me straight into her sitting room.

"How's Harold been today?" I asked, genuinely interested in the health of my friend's husband.

"The doctor's just left; Harold's pills don't seem to be agreeing with him. Can I get you a drink?"

"No thanks, just dropped in for a chat, I have so much to tell you."

I started to relay the events of the last few days, beginning with my belief that Stephen Hamilton murdered Ernest Reed and concluding with my visit to Mrs. Norton. Flo sat flabbergasted throughout.

"How could you visit that woman, Kate?" she began at last. "She would have seen you sent to prison for murder for heaven's sake!"

"I know, but I wasn't and she is on trial and I still don't believe she did it. I promised her I'd try and find the elusive man with a beard." Flo looked at me with disbelief and shook her head. "I believe her, Flo. I have been racking my brains to think of anyone I know or if I've seen a stranger around the village with facial hair, but nobody comes to mind, apart from the vicar, can you think of anyone?"

Flo sighed. "I'm sorry Kate, but I'm not going to have sleepless nights over this. I know I don't sound caring and in truth I don't care, at least not in this case. I'm convinced, like everyone else, that she killed him – she simply has to accept the consequences of her vile actions." Flo rose in agitation from her chair and began to move in earnest towards the door. "Are you sure I can't get you a drink?" Then, all of a sudden, she stopped dead and turned, a look of absolute horror washing over her face, as a realisation dawned on her. "Oh my god, he had a beard!"

"Who had a beard?" I screeched as Flo began to pace up and down wildly.

"He was sitting in the car while I talked to your mother, the day before the murder, yes he definitely had a beard, Jack Palmer – that's who!"

CHAPTER 26 – ANOTHER ONE FOR THE ALBUM

"Jack Palmer! Of course, it makes sense when you think about it. If Jack, not mother, had received a letter telling him to confess to something he had done in the past, a past none of us apart from mother knows very little about, he probably wouldn't have been very happy, would he? That's why they decided to drive up here that day. Then, if he had been led to believe from talk around the village, that Doctor Daniels was the number one culprit, well he would have been very keen, to put it mildly, to speak to him. You know I never really felt safe around him, Flo."

"Careful now Kate, don't go jumping to conclusions without any real proof. Just because he had a beard when I saw him, doesn't mean he was the killer," she pointed out, trying to calm me. "After all," Flo continued, "the fact that someone else was present in the house was only on the hearsay of a distraught woman being accused of murder for god's sake." She was right, of course.

"Ok ... what's the best thing to do?" I thought aloud. "Evidence, that's what James keeps telling me I need, evidence. Yes ..." My mind was going into overdrive for this was my first real lead; it helped that I had no love for Jack Palmer, just loathing and disgust. "I know ... I need a recent picture of him to show Mrs. Norton. I'll have to go down to the bungalow – I'll talk to Beth. Yes, I'll ask Beth to drive me down." I realised now I was sounding manic and the look on Flo's face certainly conveyed a feeling of concern about my mental state.

"Kate," she said at last, with acceptance in her tone, "whatever you do, please, just be very careful, my dear girl."

I hugged her as I left before turning my back and striding out towards my flat. It was strange, I thought, that even though mother had never shown me any real compassion over the years, I suddenly felt a feeling of some relief in my conviction that Jack was the evil part of their partnership and she was completely innocent; after all, she was still my mother. Had I finally found it in me to forgive her? Whether I was right or just being naive, time would soon tell.

A plan was forming in my head, if only I could locate the envelope containing my provisional driving licence. Yes, there it was lying deep at the bottom of a pile of 'to deal with' correspondence – I had made up my mind to ask Beth for a driving lesson.

***

"You've got to be kidding," was her immediate response, "drive all the bloody way down to the bungalow to take a ruddy picture, with you at the wheel. Are you insane?" I had obviously caught her at a bad moment.

"I don't think you fully understand the urgency, Beth: he might have been the one who murdered Doctor Daniels. How about a cup of tea? I'll put the kettle on."

It took several cups, and a large slice of Victoria sandwich, to convince her that a trip to the coast was actually a good idea. However, she did manage to persuade me to overturn my original suggestion of a driving lesson (pointing out her nerves were bad enough as she had had very little sleep due to the fact that Christopher was teething) before putting forward an alternative, more plausible proposal of her own. She and Ben would take Christopher on a trip to see his granny (how mother hated being called granny; Beth admitted to me she actually enjoyed watching her squirm at the mention of the word) and, whilst there, they would innocently take a few family photos for the album.

The following afternoon, subsequent to a quick call to mother to inform her of their unscheduled visit, Beth and Ben together with a screaming baby Christopher, safely secured in his car seat, drew up in front of mother's seaside love nest. A striking building that sat comfortably in a quiet cul-de-sac.

Mother seemed a little nervous at their appearance, but invited them straight into her large, recently installed, immaculate kitchen, where she had set out afternoon tea.

"I must say I was surprised to hear from you Ben, especially in the middle of the week. Everything alright; your father, is he well?" she asked as she poured out three cups of steaming hot Earl Grey into her best fine china.

"Yes, no problems, quiet time of the year at the farm as you know. Christopher has been a bit off colour, hasn't he, Beth? The poor mite's teething; we're up with him most nights at the moment." Beth looked anxiously around her.

"Jack out, is he?" she asked.

"Jack's at the snooker hall again; don't know when

he'll be home."

Mother's manner and voice showed irritation at the absence of her other half. Damn, thought Beth, what the hell do I do now; he might not be back for hours? To be honest, she had never been comfortable in mother's company, which is one reason Ben was more than a little surprised and suspicious when Beth suggested a trip to see her. However, he loved and trusted his wife and if she felt an outing was necessary then who was he to argue?

"Shall we retreat into the lounge; I've put all my precious things out of Christopher's reach, so he can play about safely on the carpet."

Two hours later and the strained conversation had finally come to a complete halt and the lights were beginning to turn on in the street outside. Beth knew she could not drag their stay out much longer, when finally, to her relief; the front door opened and the sound of Jack staggering into the hall brought unusual joy to her ears.

"Visitors, you didn't tell me your beloved son was coming, Rosemary darling. Ben, Beth and, oh yes, little Christopher, how absolutely tickety-boo," he mused as he exploded into the room. The sarcasm in his speech was obvious and so too was the bushy red beard that covered his face. Ben was the first to remark on its magnificence as he rose to his feet to shake his hand.

"Wow, Jack, that's some beard, given up shaving have we?" Ben mocked as Jack rubbed at his facial fuzz with obvious satisfaction.

"The ladies love it, son, they absolutely love it," and with that he lurched at a startled Beth and, before the poor girl could do anything to stop him, gave her a full-on smooch, from which she just about controlled herself from heaving. "You loved that, didn't you girl?" He grinned, patting her bottom before grabbing her around the waist.

Beth felt repulsed at his spontaneous act and more than a little angry with her husband for not remarking on it, but she remembered why they were there and managed to extricate herself from Jack's grasp.

"Unfortunately it's getting late and we must be going, but before we do how about a family photo? I was looking through our pictures the other day and realised we haven't had one taken together for months."

It took Ben a few minutes to set up the digital camera, which gave granny an opportunity to glam up a bit, before, several clicks later, Beth had the evidence she had come for.

***

"Are you going to tell me now what the hell that was all about, Beth?" Ben demanded as she drove for home with Christopher now thankfully sound asleep in the back seat.

"Kate was the one who wanted a photo, ask her," she replied curtly, "more importantly why didn't you say anything when that creep mauled me?"

"Jack's harmless enough," remarked Ben, to Beth's growing annoyance. "What if I was to grow a beard, do you think it would suit me?" He posed gazing at his face carefully in the vanity mirror.

"Over my dead body!" she screamed, abruptly ending their conversation.

***

Sometime later, standing at the door to my flat, I stared in revulsion at the evil being bouncing my little nephew on his knee.

"Good photos?" Startled, I spun around quickly, only to be unexpectedly confronted by James.

"Sorry, didn't mean to scare you. It's my break, thought I'd spend some time with my favourite girl."

It was a bit surreal kissing James in his uniform and even, I thought, a tiny bit naughty. Once in my flat, I prepared us something to eat while explaining to him about the pictures. He seemed impressed at my ingenuity and took the camera to get the prints made up at work.

I had managed to fix up another visit to see Mrs. Norton for the following day; thankfully, Laura had agreed to me taking more time off. Coincidently, Molly was due to see her as well, so we arranged to meet up beforehand in a pub near the prison for a catch up.

"You continue to surprise me, Kate, but I must say I do admire your take on the situation. Mrs. Norton is very lucky to have you on her side after what she tried to do to you."

"What do you think of her chances of getting off?" I asked as I showed her the photos of Jack.

"Well we had a long chat yesterday and I've been over all the information the police have allowed me to see. I think it boils down to these pictures: if Jack was the man at Lime House, to be honest it's probably the only chance she has."

Mrs. Norton greeted us both with genuine warmth. I believed that at last she felt she had someone on her side. Eagerly, I reached into my pocket and produced the photos with growing anticipation of her positive reaction. She stared at the images for some time and then handed them back to me, her eyes filling with tears.

"Well?" I cried. "Is this the man who killed Doctor Daniels?"

Mrs. Norton dabbed at her cheeks. "I want to say yes but I can't; I can't be certain, I'm so sorry."

It was me who was sorry; I was so confident I had got it right, I had raised the poor woman's hopes for them only to be taken away again.

CHAPTER 27 – THE TRIAL BEGINS

The excited twittering in the packed gallery soon gave way to silence as the judge and the twelve carefully picked jurors took their seats. It had now been over two months since the murder and, surrounded by family and friends, I looked around at the eager eyes of the numerous members of the public (many of them familiar faces) and reporters, waiting fervently for the first glimpse of the accused.

Mrs. Norton, her head bowed, entered the historic, wood-panelled courtroom, flanked by two female officers. As she took her place in the dock, a low muttering broke out around the room. Judge Pendleton, a round, ruddy-faced gentleman, a pair of metal-framed glasses balancing delicately on the end of his nose, called for order before his opening question, which he addressed directly to Mrs. Norton.

"Mrs. Phyllis Norton, you are here today accused of the murder of Doctor Michael Daniels, how do you plead?"

"Not guilty, your honour," her voice trembled as she answered honestly. I felt ashamed, after all this time I realised it had never crossed my mind to ask Mrs. Norton her first name – Phyllis, it suited her.

There followed opening remarks from both the prosecutor, Lionel Henderson, a middle-aged man with nicotine stained fingers – the result I assumed of heavy smoking – and Molly, both of whom were dressed in a black gown and wig.

The first to take the stand for the prosecution was the coroner, to ascertain cause of death. Without any hesitation, he revealed he had discovered the doctor's own teeth had left imprints on his lips, indicating something had been held over his mouth; in other words, he had been suffocated. An indentation at the side of his skull also confirmed he had been subjected to several violent blows to the head. A large onyx paperweight, found by forensics in the study, was shown to the jury and recorded as evidence – the coroner confirmed it had been instrumental in the killing of Doctor Daniels. These chilling disclosures caused a muffled gasp amongst the assembly.

Up next in the witness box, I naturally felt uneasy as I swore to tell the truth and nothing but the truth. It had been inevitable I should be called for the prosecution; after all, I had been the first suspect in this heinous crime. Relating my story to the gawping gathering seemed to go on for hours. The questions and my answers that came afterwards, I soon realised, did little to help Phyllis's cause, even I thought: 'who would believe she was not guilty?' by the time the prosecutor had finished with me. Predictably, he brought up the subject of the poisoned pen letters, the motive, he alleged, for Doctor Daniels murder. Incensed by his presumption, I spoke with determination of my conviction.

"I'm sorry, I've said this before, as far as I am aware there is no evidence to show that Doctor Daniels was the writer of those letters; it would have been out of character. The doctor was a good man, a healer."

I glared around at the faces now focused on me, knowing the majority believed Doctor Daniels to be guilty of that particular crime. Resuming my place between James and father, I listened with a sinking feeling to the evidence of several more witnesses from around the village. The growing facts, being transmitted by the prosecution, were definitely supporting the guilty judgement against Phyllis, who was listening from her place in the dock with a mounting expression of despair on her face. Even Molly's undeniably skilled cross-examination of the witnesses sadly did little to raise my hopes of a not guilty verdict.

With the first day of the trial over, Phyllis managed a weak smile in my direction, before being escorted back to her cell.

Over the following week, the evidence continued to stack up against her. Chief Inspector Wheeler was able to confirm the only fingerprints found on the paperweight belonged to Phyllis. He had gone on to explain further that several items, identified as belonging to the doctor by his sons, had been found hidden in Phyllis's room. The forensic team had also discovered a torn-up letter, discarded in an outside dustbin, accusing her of stealing. Remarking on my outburst concerning the letters, the chief inspector pointed out that I had been correct when I said they had not been able to obtain any real evidence to verify the doctor was the writer, in fact, his computer had proved to be completely void of any criminal activity. I was thankful he had been able to make that declaration in such a public arena; now perhaps the gossips would turn their attention elsewhere.

Four more gruelling days later and, if the reporting in the newspapers was to be believed, Phyllis's bleak cell was to be her home for the foreseeable future. It was Friday at last and the weekend loomed in front of us, a welcome break for everyone. Arriving back at Willow Green, after yet another torturous day in court, father suggested we all go to the Bull for a drink and something to eat – his treat. Naturally, the main topic was the trial, so I was actually relieved when I felt the vibration of my mobile phone.

"Hope I'm not disturbing your dinner; just had to let you know, I've called your mother and Jack Palmer as witnesses." Molly's voice sounded weary.

"Right, good …" I hesitated before going on, "how do you think it's going?"

"Not as well as I had hoped, but don't worry, Kate, I'm feeling positive and that's what I've told Phyllis. Today was the final one for the prosecution; Monday will be my turn. I'll be calling her to the stand first thing; at last it'll be her chance to tell everybody exactly what took place. So far, the subject of someone else being present hasn't been disclosed and that's exactly how I wanted to play it, trust me." I did trust her, really I did.

***

The weekend passed in a blur; I felt all talked out. James came round on Sunday evening and we simply sat watching television, enjoying the closeness of each other, when the phone rang. It was Flo.

"Sorry Kate, I know it's late, but I wanted to catch you before we went to court tomorrow, I thought I might not get a chance to speak to you there. It's Harold…"

"Is he ok?"

"Oh, yes … he's actually better at the moment, the

new pills seem to be working. No ..., he's asked me to ask you and James if you wouldn't mind popping round tomorrow evening about six."

How peculiar. In all these years I could only remember having a handful of conversations with Harold, mainly about gardening, and now out of the blue he was asking me round for a chat.

"Do you know what he wants to talk to us about, Flo?"

"No, I think it might be about the trial; he has been a bit agitated all week ... yes, I think it's about the trial."

I looked at James and he nodded. "Yes, that'll be fine, tell Harold not to worry, we'll be there."

***

Monday morning and the courtroom was packed yet again, with standing room only in the gallery. Molly Brightman rose to address the judge and the jury. "Ladies and gentlemen, you have heard the case for the prosecution, now it is time to hear from the woman being accused of this dreadful crime." Phyllis Norton took her place in the witness box looking tired and drawn; her deeply-lined features making her look older than her years. "Mrs. Norton, would you please tell the court in your own words what happened on the day Doctor Daniels died."

Taking a deep breath, Phyllis began her story. When she got to the part where the man with the beard had come to the house; a low muttering quickly encircled the room. Concluding her account, she asked for a glass of water.

"Phyllis," began Molly gently, "thank you for

telling the court so clearly what took place that dreadful day. There are a couple of questions, however, I would like to ask you. First of all: why do you think your fingerprints were the only ones found on the murder weapon if, as you say, this mystery man killed the doctor?"

"Well ... I suppose because I had cleaned the study the day before, and had to move the paper weight to polish the desk, and I've already told you the man was wearing gloves so he wouldn't have left any fingerprints, would he?"

"I see, yes, of course. When the forensic team examined the scene they found the tea and biscuits you had prepared and one of the cups was empty; did the man drink from the cup?"

"He might've I wasn't really that concerned about the tea; the doctor was lying there dead, for god's sake." Molly handed her a tissue to dry her eyes.

"No further questions, your honour."

Lionel Henderson got slowly to his feet with the look of a predator about to leap on its prey. He began to quiz Phyllis on her evidence, twisting and turning her story until it seemed she had no fight left in her. His attack completed, she vacated the witness box, obviously exhausted. Alas, I was unsure if Phyllis's appearance had the desired effect Molly had wanted. While the court adjourned for lunch, I managed a quick word with her.

"Boy, that was brutal; Phyllis looked shattered."

"It was much as I had expected; Henderson's got a bit of a reputation for being a bully in and out of the courtroom apparently. I had warned Phyllis, I think she coped well in the circumstances."

I was not entirely convinced. "Has mother and

Jack arrived yet?"

"Yes, they're waiting in the witness waiting rooms. I didn't want them anywhere near the courtroom this morning while Phyllis was giving her evidence. By the way, I'm calling your mother first thing after lunch."

***

Mother took the stand dressed completely inappropriately for the time of year and the occasion, in a floral low-cut dress, just as if she was attending a garden party. On her obviously recently-coloured, auburn hair, sitting to one side of her head, a pink fascinator completed her ensemble.

"Mrs. Rosemary Oliver, I understand you were visiting Willow Green on the day Doctor Daniels was murdered, can you tell the court exactly why you were in the village?"

Mother turned to face the judge. "Your honour, my name is Ms Rosemary Weston; I reverted to my maiden name after my divorce." The judge peered at her over his glasses.

"Hum … thank you, Ms Weston, but would you please address your answers to Ms Brightman."

"Oh sorry, your honour, how silly of me; I've never been in court before, you see."

I looked over at father who rolled his eyes at mother's obvious flirtatious attempt to charm the judge, while Beth nudged me hard in the ribs.

"My apologies, Ms Weston," Molly stated, before continuing, "now can you please answer my question: why were you in the village that day?"

"I was simply visiting my children, that's not a crime, is it?" Once again, mother focused her gaze on the judge.

"No, of course, it is commendable that you would want to see your children, but I was under the impression you were in the village because you had received a nasty letter, accusing you of some sort of crime, have I been wrongly informed?"

"Totally, I'm a law-abiding citizen and I'm incensed that you would believe to the contrary." Molly persisted in her questioning, but mother continued to deny she had received any such letter, virtually calling me a liar in front of everyone. What game was she playing? Of course, it was true that neither Flo nor I had actually seen a letter. Nevertheless, did I want the chance to retake the stand, in order to uphold my integrity, because in the end, it would simply be my word against mother's? Sadly, what difference would it actually make to the outcome of this rapidly increasing farce of a trial?

"Thank you, Ms Weston, I have no more questions."

No more questions, but it was obvious, to me anyway, that mother was lying. Where was Molly going with all this? Down a deep hole, it seemed, and taking Phyllis with her. Unsurprisingly, the prosecutor had no questions to ask her; in fact, I thought his demeanour had become slightly smug.

Beaming confidently, mother took her place at the rear of the courtroom, adjusting her fascinator while she waited for the entrance of her lover. Jack Palmer, for once looking smart in a suit and tie, strode to his place in the witness box.

"He's shaved his beard," whispered Beth under her breath.

"Yes, I had noticed."

"Jack Palmer, you are the partner of Ms Rosemary Weston, are you not?" Molly's opening question seemed to amuse him.

"If that's what she's calling herself these days, then, yes, we live together."

"I understand you were visiting Willow Green on the day of Doctor Daniels death; can you tell the court why you were there?" I could see Jack's eyes scanning the room, trying to locate mother.

"We were visiting Rosemary's daughter, Kate."

"I see, and was this something you did on a regular basis, visiting Kate Oliver, I mean?"

"Hell no, they hate the sight of each other."

"So, why were you there at that particular time, was it perhaps because Rosemary had received a nasty letter, accusing her of a crime, and you had driven all the way just to find out who wrote it?"

Jack's voice thundered out in response. "No! I saw no letter, as I said we were just visiting." Molly looked up towards Phyllis who nodded in her direction. I realised almost at once what that meant: she had recognised Jack's voice and now Molly had the confirmation she had been pushing for.

"Let me tell you, Mr. Palmer, what I believe happened that day. I think Rosemary Weston received a letter in the post on the Thursday morning which annoyed her and you drove together to the village to try and find out who wrote it." Molly held up several statements from residents confirming that Rosemary Weston had been inquiring into the name of the poisoned pen writer. "I would like these statements recorded as evidence, your honour." Molly turned back to Jack.

"On the Friday morning, you went round to Kate

Oliver's flat and, while you waited outside in the car, Rosemary Weston interrogated her daughter about the letters. Before she left, she overheard a message from Doctor Daniels, asking her daughter to his house to collect some photos. I believe this triggered a belief in Rosemary Weston that Doctor Daniels was the writer. She then persuaded you to go round to see him, in order to confront him about her suspicions and retrieve any evidence he had against her. He probably wouldn't have recognised you but, to be sure, you wore dark glasses. I believe you had an argument with the doctor and, in a frenzied moment, brutally killed him. Then, after being discovered by the housekeeper, Phyllis Norton, you threatened to kill her too, unless she helped you incriminate Kate Oliver, on whom you wanted revenge for her continued rejection of your sexual advances."

Jack jumped to his feet and punched the air. "What rubbish! You have no evidence to back this sick theory of yours; you have no evidence because I wasn't bloody there I tell you!"

"Please sit down, Mr. Palmer," insisted the judge.

"Actually, Mr. Palmer, I do have evidence: evidence that will not only prove you were in the house that day, but will also convict you of the murder of Doctor Daniels. By the way, what happened to your beard?"

"Beard? You can see for yourself I'm clean-shaven."

Molly opened a folder and produced the pictures Beth had taken the previous month. "Do you deny these are pictures of you and Rosemary Weston's grandchild?"

Jack looked towards Beth, his gaze burning into

her.

"Can I get you a glass of water, Mr. Palmer?"

While he slowly sipped the liquid, Molly resumed her interrogation. "Did you know, Mr. Palmer, that forensics have come a long way in recent years? This glass, for instance, is now covered in your DNA, and I am confident it will match the DNA found on the tea cup you drank from after you murdered Doctor Daniels!"

The courtroom erupted, bringing the trial to a temporary halt.

"Order, order, I will not have this behaviour in my courtroom," Judge Pendleton demanded as he brought his gavel down hard on the bench. Obviously freaked out by Molly's disclosures, Jack began his confession with some eagerness.

"Ok, I admit it, I was there, but I didn't kill the old man; I've never killed anyone in my life."

An unexpected roar from the back of the room caused us all to turn round.

"Shut the fuck up, you ignorant bastard! Just shut the fuck up!"

"Sorry, Rosemary darling, but I'm not going down again on my own for you."

There was pandemonium in the room.

"Order, order!" bellowed the judge, before commanding: "please remove Ms Weston from my courtroom!"

CHAPTER 28 – DISCLOSURES

We were all in a complete state of shock as we watched mother being escorted from our sight, screaming and shouting profanities I had never heard in my life before. Ben, father, Beth and I held each other for comfort, not sure what to do next. Had we understood correctly; had Jack just told everyone mother was a murderer?

The elevated voice of Judge Pendleton trying to bring tranquillity back into the room eventually put an end to the mayhem around us.

"Ms Brightman and Mr. Henderson, would you please approach the bench?"

Molly and Lionel Henderson, both still looking stunned by Jack's unanticipated disclosure, stood side by side in front of the judge.

"Ms Brightman, do you wish to question Mr. Palmer any further, in the light of his testimony?"

"Yes your honour, unless Mr. Henderson has any objections. I think Mr. Palmer needs to explain his allegation and, in view of what he has already divulged to the court, I hope you agree, my client should be exonerated of the charge of murder."

"Let's not jump too far ahead of ourselves, Ms Brightman, but I must admit, I would be very interested to hear what Mr. Palmer has to say." Lionel Henderson raised no objections before smiling a defeated smile and returning to his seat.

"Mr. Palmer, you said something about not going

down again without Rosemary Weston, does that mean you've been in prison?"

"Yes I have … I might as well tell you … you would find out anyway. I knew Rosemary back in London you see, we were young lovers, in fact we got engaged, but she never told her parents; they would have freaked out. She was wild, loved the thrill of doing bad things, always goading me to steal for her or thumping someone because they had annoyed her. She saw this ring in a jewellers, went on about it for months, pick, pick, picking at me to get it for her. Eventually, of course, I gave in. The plan was for her to distract the jeweller while I nicked the ring, but it all went horribly wrong when his wife came in from the back of the shop, saw me, and started yelling. Rosemary managed to get away but the jeweller made a grab at me, I whacked him one and he fell over and cracked his head open. Before I could get out of the shop, the police arrived and I was arrested. I got ten years – I had previous you see, although I was let out in eight for good behaviour."

"So, Rosemary was never caught, leaving her to get married and have children while you languished in prison; that must have been very hard for you to take?" suggested Molly.

"We lost contact, she never visited me or wrote, so I didn't even know she was married until I came out and went looking for her. When we met up again, the lust we had for each other was rekindled." I looked over at father, who was seething with the realisation of the true character of his ex-wife, who had deemed to bring such a monstrous man into the bosom of his family.

"Thank you, Mr. Palmer, for an insight into your

relationship with Rosemary Weston, but now, perhaps you can tell the court exactly what happened when you went to see Doctor Daniels."

"You know most of it already; what you don't know is when Mrs. Norton left to post the letter, I let Rosemary in through the window in the doctor's study – she didn't want to come in the conventional route because she knew Mrs. Norton would recognise her. He was surprised to see her I can tell you; I think they must have had some sort of history between them because the old boy seemed … well … terrified. He completely denied writing any letter but Rosemary didn't believe him, she started ranting and raving she would ruin him. I had never seen her like that before; she was completely out of control. I tried to make her calm down, but she wasn't listening. It was then she picked up the paperweight on the desk and slammed it into his skull; she hit him again and again. In the end, I managed to pull her away, but then he started moaning … I couldn't believe he was still alive; we stood and stared at him for over a minute, before Rosemary grabbed a cushion and held it over his face. She lay with the full weight of her body on top of him, until he stopped twitching."

A terrible hush had descended upon the gathering, until slowly the sound of uncontrolled weeping from those around me began to fill the air. Jeremy and Graham Daniels, their heads in their hands, were rocking backwards and forwards in their seats, understandably completely distraught. To think my mother had caused so much anguish.

Then to my amazement, from out of nowhere, the spirit of Doctor Daniels appeared behind Jack, a smile illuminating his face. He stared towards me and nodded, as if to acknowledge that at last he had retribution. I wanted to shout aloud, to let everyone know he was with us but, of course, I could not utter a word. Slowly, as I watched, his spirit faded and then in a blink of an eye he was gone.

"Mr. Jack Palmer," Judge Pendleton began, "you will be taken from my courtroom and remanded in custody, to be tried at a later date." Turning to Phyllis, he beamed, "Mrs. Phyllis Norton, you are free to go."

I should have been ecstatic with the not guilty verdict passed on Phyllis, but any thought of celebration had been wiped from my mind. My own mother had blood on her hands; how, as a family, were we ever going to get over this?

"Come on, let's get out of here," father urged, gathering us together, trying to protect us from the horrified glances now fixed in our direction. Fighting our way out into the open air, we managed to locate father's Land Rover quickly and were soon heading back towards Willow Green.

"Look, we've all got to support each other, we can't let mother's evil actions taint us," I began, breaking the silence.

"Kate's right, none of us suspected anything, I mean …" Beth was obviously struggling to get her thoughts out.

"You never loved her, Kate, why don't you just come out and say it? How rotten she was, how bad she was …" I had not seen my brother cry since he was a young child. "How could she have done such a terrible thing?" Understandably, he was angry, angry with our mother who he had always defended against the rest of the family.

"What about nana and grandad?" I asked. "Who's

going to let them know? It will kill them."

"I'll go round to see them later, it's not something I would want to tell them over the phone. Are you coming back to the farm, Kate?" Father asked as we reached the outskirts of the village.

"I can't I'm afraid; I'm meeting James – Flo's asked us round, can't really get out of it." A sombre group dropped me at the entrance to my flat and straight into the arms of James, who I had texted about the outcome of the trial. I was thankful for a strong shoulder on which to finally relieve my distress.

***

Just before six, we arrived in front of Flo's house where she greeted us warmly. "Are you ok, my dear girl? It was so awful, I still can't believe it no one expected it."

"Still in shock really," I admitted quietly. Flo led us into her front room where, unexpectedly, other guests had already assembled: Harold, looking rather frail and half the man he used to be, was sitting majestically by the fire, a woollen blanket covering his legs.

"I think you know everyone," Flo pointed out. Indeed we did. Feeling slightly awkward, we greeted the Reverend George Stanton, Chief Inspector Wheeler, and Detective Sergeant Peters, with a handshake – wondering why we had all been summoned here.

With his breathing sounding rather laboured, Harold cleared his throat before beginning. "Thank you all for coming especially as I understand it's been a pretty horrendous day for you, Kate. Before I start, I want you all to know that Flo is completely oblivious to everything I'm about to tell you." Intrigued by his opening remarks, I sat down on the chair opposite him. "Well, I'm simply just going to come out with it: I'm the writer of the letters that have been circulating the village."

We all looked at each other in utter astonishment and disbelief. Detective Sergeant Peters took out his note pad and started scribbling madly, while Flo, who was just bringing in a tray of refreshments, managed to put it down safely before collapsing onto the settee.

"Harold, no!" she wailed, as I scurried to her side.

"I'm so sorry Flo, but it's true. James, there's a box file just behind you, would you place it on the table please. If you look inside, you will find the copies of the nineteen letters I have sent, together with the evidence I have collected over the years."

"But why, Harold? For god's sake, why?" Flo cried in anguish.

"Because, my dear, I have done some bad things in my life and I have witnessed bad things too, and with my time rapidly running out, I wanted to come clean and give others the push perhaps they needed to do the same thing. How wrong I was to believe in the integrity of the human race."

"Yes, unfortunately Harold, you have caused a great deal of stress amongst my parishioners," imparted the Reverend Stanton, who was helping me to comfort Flo.

"Perhaps sir, you could begin at the beginning. Peters here will write down your statement." Chief Inspector Wheeler affirmed, while Harold adjusted his position in his chair.

"I have rehearsed what I'm about to tell you so many times in my head, it almost seems surreal to be telling you now. When I look back at my life, well, it seemed to fall apart when my lad Brian died. He was the apple of my eye you see, with his cheeky smile and so much energy; it was difficult to keep up with him. When the lord took him away, I wanted to die too. I was numb for years. Flo and me, well we just existed; I still loved her, still do, but I found it impossible to show it. I kept busy with my jobs around the village, I especially liked working for Doctor Daniels who was always appreciative, that's why I feel particularly ashamed. He used to leave his paperwork everywhere and I'm sorry to say I took advantage of my position and read documents I shouldn't have. Then I got a job working for the Hamilton's. I've no excuse for my behaviour Flo, please don't hate me, I did try to resist her, but she was bloody persistent ... Mrs. Barbara Hamilton." Harold's voice almost sounded venomous in tone.

"We had an affair for about three months. I say 'affair', but it wasn't love you understand, just sex, plain and simple. Then she ended it, without even a discussion." Harold looked forlornly towards Flo, knowing how much pain he was causing her. "I carried on working there; we needed the money. When I saw she was pregnant, I began to wonder if it was mine but nothing was ever said, so I said nothing. Stephen was obviously a wrong 'un from the start: got up to all sorts he did, nothing like my lad in that respect, except for his eyes; they both had my eyes, so I knew, but I still never said. I caught him stealing tools from me on several occasions and on the night

Ernest Reed died, I came across my old spanner on the ground outside the pub where Ernest had left his bike against the wall. Later, when I heard the news of Ernest's death, I suspected Stephen had used it to loosen the old boy's wheels; don't ask me why, but to my shame I never said anything. James, there's an envelope in the inbox marked 'SH'; in it you'll find the spanner," he turned to the chief inspector, "I hope his fingerprints are still on there, he should answer for what he did."

Of course, the revelation that Stephen was the cause of Ernest's death was not exactly news to James and me, but at least now, we knew how he did it.

"I don't believe it, I really don't believe it; Harold, you know how Emily suffered when her father died, my god, man, he was your friend!" The Reverend Stanton was now pacing rapidly up and down the room. "I found his body, stiff and cold in that ditch, it still haunts me to this day. Manslaughter, that's what Stephen Hamilton should be charged with, manslaughter!"

"Ok, sir, please calm yourself. Be assured we will get this spanner tested as soon as we get back to the station and if Stephen Hamilton's fingerprints are on it, he will be called in for questioning." Absorbing the chief inspector's words, Reverend Stanton managed to compose himself.

While the focus was directed away from her, Flo leaned in towards me and whispered, "The spirits were right then," before rising and taking her place by Harold's side, putting her hand lovingly in his, a gesture to reassure her husband she forgave him.

"Well, we had better be going Harold, it's been a long day," I pointed out as James and I began to put on our coats.

"Oh sorry, I've not finished yet, there's something else and it involves you Kate, please sit down, please," Harold coaxed. Reluctantly, we resumed our seats.

"I want to take you back some twenty years when I was a gardener at your farm. It was a beautiful garden and I was very proud to work in it. I think you were about five. I had been looking at them bluebells of your mother's for a while; they were wilting see, so I thought I'd try to perk them up a bit."

"I remember that day only too well: mother went mad when you started digging."

"Yes, that's right. I had only myself to blame of course; she had told me to leave them, but I had my reputation as a gardener to consider. When I started to dig, my little doggy helper joined me."

"Oh yes, little Penny, she was so cute."

"Yes, poor thing, your mother kicked her, do you recall that? Well, later, before it got dark, I sneaked back and started to refill the hole the little mite had dug and that's when I found it: the locket. I recognised it almost immediately as belonging to that au pair of yours, Gabrielle, the one that went missing."

"Gabrielle," I screamed, jumping to my feet, "what are you saying, Harold?"

"I'm saying ... perhaps Gabrielle is buried under the bluebells. In my letter to your mother, I had accused her of murder. To be absolutely honest, it was only a gut feeling, but knowing now she is definitely capable of such a crime, I think my instincts could be right."

"No, please no, James, it can't be true, I can't breathe, please James, say it can't be true." I was devastated. Was it possible; was Gabrielle lying buried in our garden?

"Right, now we're all well aware of how Ms Weston reacted after receiving that letter, which obviously must have had some truth in it, I think it would be an idea to get a forensic team out to the farm to examine the site straight away. I'll make a few phone calls, if you would excuse me." Chief Inspector Wheeler immediately left the room.

Nothing could have prepared me for the emotional roller coaster I had been riding on that day – I was a mess both physically and mentally.

"I think we could all do with a stiff drink, don't you?" So, while Flo searched for the bottle of brandy she kept just for Christmas, I carefully opened the envelope marked 'G' and gently lifted from it the locket that had hung around Gabrielle's neck, all those years ago. The two miniature pictures of Alita and me, now only just recognisable, still lay within their delicate frames.

"Perhaps she had just dropped it James, when we were playing, perhaps she just dropped it."

"Darling, I hope that's the case, but we need to be sure, you do understand that." James took me in his arms as I began to sob uncontrollably.

"Right, Peters and Constable Robinson: would you both go ahead to the farm and inform the occupants about the turn of events? I will follow as quickly as I can with the forensic team."

Of course, I was not going to be left behind, but as I prepared to leave, Harold called be back into the room.

"Kate, there's one more thing. I actually wrote twenty letters," he whispered so only I could hear, before reaching down the side of his chair from where he carefully brought to the surface the folded sheet, which completed the poisoned correspondence. "This one was to Louise: I want you to put it in the fire. If you see her, tell her I was mistaken," said Harold, recalling the image from his son's bedroom window, of Louise, standing before the well at the bottom of her garden, a small blooded bundle clasped tightly in her arms.

I stared into the flames as the paper shrivelled, crumbled and burned into nothingness, wondering just for a split second what Louise had done to initiate Harold putting pen to paper – now no one apart from Harold and Louise would ever know.

CHAPTER 29 – A SECRET PLACE

The habitual chimes of the grandfather clock, which had stood in the hall at Hill Farm long before I was born, informed us it was midnight – a time when most mortals should be tucked up warm in bed, not waiting with growing desolation as to the outcome of a police investigation taking place in their very own garden.

A swarm of officers, together with a forensic team dressed from head to toe in overalls, had arrived at the farm, and quickly cordoned off the area where they proposed to carry out an excavation. A large white tent had been erected, emitting an eerie glow into the night sky, while the silhouettes of those working carefully within its walls, could clearly be seen by the outside observer.

My family and I had been asked to wait in the house – what an excruciating wait it was proving to be. My mind was in such turmoil, I thought it would explode; if Gabrielle was buried out there, was it mother's doing? Had she killed her in a fit of anger and buried her beneath the bluebells, carrying on with her life as if nothing had happened? I had been so inaccurate with my reasoning over Doctor Daniels' murder; I prayed I was wrong again. The eventual appearance of Chief Inspector Wheeler drained from me whatever colour I had left.

"I have to inform you: we have uncovered human remains. It will be a while before they can be taken away for examination; I'm afraid I can't even tell you at this juncture whether they are male or female. I suggest you all try and get some rest, it's going to be a long night."

Ronny, obviously concerned at my distress, put a comforting arm around me.

"Come on everyone, he's right, we're all exhausted after everything that's happened today, I think we should all try and get some rest," father insisted.

"I would like to go back to the village and get some of my things first, if that's ok?" I asked, drying my tears.

Immediately, Beth picked up her car keys. "I'll run you there; James is obviously tied up and, quite frankly, I could do with the distraction – if that's ok with you, Ben?" Hardly waiting for Ben's reply, we exited the room.

***

The full moon was slipping effortlessly behind the growing clouds as we began the drive along the lanes heading down towards Willow Green. The headlights of the car cast dancing shadows amongst the winter hedgerows, where night creatures scurried for safety. Suddenly, from out of nowhere, a vehicle loomed behind us, its powerful beam of intense light blindingly reflected into the rear view mirror.

"What the hell does he think he's playing at – idiot. Come on then, pass, if you're in so much of a hurry!" shouted Beth to the unknown driver, before slowing slightly, allowing them to overtake. Alarmingly, the vehicle hovered alongside us for a few moments before pulling away at top speed. "Wonder what their problem was?"

Minutes later, we arrived in the village.

"Don't be too long, I'll wait for you in the car." Keeping the engine running, Beth hummed quietly to herself, trying to evade the morbid images entering her head, while I quickly gathered a few things from my flat. Opening my overnight bag, I packed clothes for a few days before picking up what I really had come back for: Gabrielle's jewellery box. Lovingly, I wrapped my precious gift in a jumper and placed it within the case. Back out into the darkness I opened the passenger door and quickly settled into my seat.

"Cor, it's cold out there, glad you kept the engine running," I looked over at Beth, who had a fixed stare on her face. "Are you ok? Are you mad with me? I wasn't that long ... Beth?"

"I think Beth has been a little disturbed by my appearance."

Alarmed at the sound of a male voice, I twisted around. Sitting in the dimness of the back seat, with that unforgettable sneer clearly on his face, sat Jack Palmer, wielding a large knife in his outstretched hand.

"Shit, how did you get here?" I shrieked in fear at the predicament in which Beth and I had found ourselves. Jack leaned forward – I could feel his stale breath on my face.

"Let's just say there are a couple of coppers who have a lot of explaining to do. Right, girls: time, I think, for a little drive. Beth, my love, I hope you're going to be a good girl and follow my instructions; I wouldn't want you to do anything stupid that would make me angry and cause me to do something unfortunate. Before we go, however, I would be grateful if you would both hand over your mobile phones."

A petrified look passed between us as Beth drove the car slowly forward and out of the village.

A mile or so into our journey, Jack ordered Beth to stop the car, whose headlights were slicing their way through the gloom, enabling us to observe the area where Beth's car had come to a standstill – an entrance to a field.

"Ok, Kate, get out and open the gate. No funny stuff, don't forget I have this rather impressive knife around your best friend's neck …"

The rutted meadow proved a difficult drive until eventually the car came to an abrupt halt – unable to manoeuvre through the muddy conditions any further. Leaping from the vehicle, Jack commanded us to get out. He tied our hands tightly with rope and produced a torch from a backpack he was carrying, and so began a terrifying march.

Through the darkness, we could just make out that we were heading towards a wooded area. Jack pushed us forward into the overgrown vegetation. Moving on into the unknown, a small clearing eventually opened up before us, in which stood a dilapidated wooden shack.

"Welcome to my country abode; sorry it's a bit basic, but it's home and it's going to be your home for the rest of your lives." His words sent a chill through our very souls.

Lighting the oil lamps scattered around the only room, it was obvious by the state of the place it had been a long time since anyone had actually lived in it.

"Bit of a mess, but I'm sure you're not worried about that. This is where Rosemary and I used to meet. Yes, it's certainly seen a lot of action, Rosemary was quite a girl when it came to sex, very experimental – the more pain, the better she liked it."

It was then I noticed, to my horror, the numerous rusting chains hanging from the overhead beams. Jack licked his lips before continuing, a strange expression appearing on his weathered features.

"I think, girls, we too can have some fun here together. What do you say?"

Standing in front of me, he ripped open my coat and eyed my body up and down with an approving leer. Leaning forward, he growled into my ear, "I can't tell you how I've dreamed of this day. I know you're going to be such a great fuck; the more you scream and fight the more I will enjoy it."

I said nothing, not even a murmur. How I hated the bastard.

"Leave her alone, you sick shit, just leave her alone!" Beth screamed hysterically.

"Oh Beth, Beth, do you feel left out? Don't worry, you can watch and when I've finished, you'll be next, you know I'm more man than that boy you're married to."

***

Waiting impatiently at the farm for our return, our family were getting anxious.

"The girls have been a long time," remarked Ben, looking at his watch, "think I'll try and ring Beth's mobile."

His call went straight through to voicemail, just as Chief Inspector Wheeler pounded on the door.

"Sorry to disturb you again, but I've had a call

from the station: apparently Jack Palmer has escaped en route to prison; knocked out two officers, almost killing one. Have your daughter and daughter-in-law got back yet?"

"No, we were beginning to get worried and now we know that creep is at large ... you don't think they could be in danger, do you?"

"Afraid so, Palmer had been ranting and raving they were the reason he got caught. It's imperative we find them before he does; god knows what he'll do."

A cavalcade of vehicles was soon en route to the village. Finding no sign of Beth's car, an urgent search began of the area.

***

Back at the shack, Jack had tied us both securely to the only bed in the room – a dilapidated metal structure that obviously had a tale or two to tell – before turning to leave.

"As much as I hate for you to wait any longer for me, I must deal with your little car out there first, before anyone notices it ... don't go away, girls."

"Did you realise the ghost of Doctor Daniels was standing behind you in the courtroom?" I began slowly, causing Jack to spin around, a quizzical expression appearing on his face. "Oh yes ... he was delighted to have justice at last."

"What's the matter with you, are you mad? Does insanity run in the family?"

"No, I'm not mad, Jack, but I can see and talk to the dead; in fact at this very moment there are several spirits in this room." Beth looked over at me alarmed.

"If you're trying to spook me, you've picked on

the wrong person," Jack snarled.

I closed my eyes; I had never prayed as hard as I did at that moment. Prayed for my spirit friends to help us – they did not disappoint.

"Kate, what's happening?" cried Beth as the entire shack was instantly flooded with light, a light which rose like a beacon into the heavens whilst at the same time from some distance away, a haunting sound growing louder by the second from a much-loved musical box drifted through the cold night air.

"I knew it: you're a bloody witch you are, a bloody witch," Jack Palmer barked before sprinting from the shack and out of our sight.

"Quick, Beth, the knife, see if we can drag the bed so you can reach it." It was much heavier than it looked. "There must be something stopping it, can you see anything your side?"

"Yes, there's a box, I'll try and kick it out of the way." Although still in a daze from her spiritual encounter, like a contortionist Beth twisted her body, until finally she managed the unmanageable and pushed away the obstacle preventing our flight to freedom. "Done. Now for the bloody knife."

Rocking the table on which Jack had placed the blade, at last with one almighty shove it fell to the floor, near enough for Beth to grab it. Managing to cut herself free, my best friend was then at last able to release me from my bondage.

"Kate, was it true what you said? Was Doctor Daniels really at the court?"

"Yes, I think his spirit is at peace at last. By the way, you were brilliant just now, didn't realise you were so strong. Look, we need to get out of here quickly, before that bastard regains his courage and comes back." Picking up a couple of the oil lamps, we stepped out into the bleak darkness.

Thrashing through the undergrowth, I took the lead through the maze of trees, until, to our relief, we came upon an unkempt hedge, seemingly the boundary dividing the wood from the road beyond. Feeling our way along the barricade preventing our flight, Beth took my hand as we made our escape over a well-worn stile; a hidden treasure amongst the dense shrubbery. Clambering over it eagerly, we began to run; run for our lives.

By now we had abandoned the failing lamps and were relying only on the moon to guide us. Approaching a bend in the road, we both let out a scream simultaneously as a tall, unwelcome figure rose unexpectedly from the murky depths of the roadside ditch – it was Jack.

"Thought you'd get away from me, did you, bitch? You didn't really scare me with that talk of ghosts."

He made a grab for me, forcing my arm high up my back and causing me to cry out in pain.

"Run, Beth, just get away, please, run!" I could tell by the look in her eyes she really did not want to leave me, "think of Christopher, please, go!"

I watched, with tears cascading down my cheeks, as my best friend disappeared reluctantly from my sight.

Without a word, Jack dragged me backwards into a break in the hedge, before throwing me roughly to the ground. I heard the alarming sound of his trouser zip opening and, before I knew it, his full weight was on top of me, pinning my unwilling body beneath his. I was unable to put up any resistance as he pulled feverishly at my undergarments, his breathing now intensified, as his whole being seemed to be taking great pleasure in what he was about to do to me. I was powerless to fight back. The man I had felt repulsion for all my life was about to rape me.

Please God, let it be over soon.

Then an amazing thing happened, for behind his head an incandescent vision appeared. I could not believe what I was seeing – it was Josh's spirit. There was no mistake. In his raised hand, a large instrument came crashing down onto Jack's skull, knocking him out cold. Pushing his unconscious body off mine, I stood and faced my saviour. Josh winked at me and blew me a kiss, before vanishing back into the night.

The headlights from approaching cars and the shouts of 'are you all right?' brought immediate joy to my ears. With my relieved family now bustling around me, including Beth, who had managed to flag down the search party, which fortunately had already been heading in our direction, I felt safe once again.

"Hey chief inspector, I thought those lights above the woods were weird enough, but look, I've just found a cricket bat, wonder how it got all the way out here?"

Climbing into father's Land Rover, I smiled knowingly to myself.

CHAPTER 30 - A LETTER FROM THE GRAVE

It had been over a month since Jack Palmer had finally had his come-uppance and been thrown into prison, with a growing list of charges which now included abduction and attempted rape. I, on the other hand, was back at work in the post office with Laura, trying to keep myself busy. I must say, the folk of Willow Green had shown my family nothing but sympathy and kindness, in fact, life was almost back to some sort of normality, except for two things: first, we were still waiting nervously for the forensic team's results on the skeleton found at the farm and second, James had insisted on moving in with me.

Living with my police officer boyfriend seemed a comforting idea when he suggested it one evening in the Bull, after we had finished off two bottles of wine between us, mainly because I was still having nightmares from my time in the woods, but reality … well, that was even better.

"This is the last load, honestly Kate," James panted as he hauled yet another box up the steps to my flat. I had not realised how much stuff, mainly clothes, James had accumulated, and where it was all going to go in my tiny one-bedroomed home, I had no idea – it was going to be a bit of a squeeze but I was sure one I was going to enjoy.

The call one evening to go to the farm was one I been dreading; the results from the forensic team were ready to be disclosed to the family. Chief Inspector Wheeler looked solemn as he began to update us.

"I can now confirm the bones are of a young female and have been in the ground about twenty years. We have been in touch with the police in France and have carried out DNA tests, I'm afraid there is no doubt they are the bones of Gabrielle Duval."

Unexpectedly, father looked more shocked than any of us.

"I'm sorry, chief inspector, but our au pair was called Gabrielle Bayne not Duval, you've got the wrong person."

"Jonathan, Gabrielle had changed her name, we found that out when we visited France. I thought we told you and Ronny," Beth declared, shocked at father's obvious distress.

"No, no I would have remembered, believe me, I would have remembered if you had told me that," father moaned, holding his head in his hands.

It was all too much: Gabrielle had said she would never leave me and she had not broken her word. I was grief-stricken, realising she had been with me all the time. Although acknowledging our anguish, the chief inspector had no option but to continue.

"Gabrielle's mother has been informed; she is making arrangements to take her remains back to France as soon as possible. I have to tell you, I have interviewed Rosemary Weston and told her of our findings but, up to now, I have not been able to obtain a confession from her. I will keep trying, because there's no doubt in my mind she's guilty of killing Gabrielle."

Hearing this latest news, Ben sprang to his feet and stormed out of the room, followed by an anxious Beth.

It was true then: our mother was a double murderer. I wanted to see the assassin; to scream and shout at her; to ask her why she had killed such a wonderful young girl, who had shown me nothing but love, and why she had felt it acceptable to destroy the life of an elderly woman, who until now had had no idea what had happened to her beautiful daughter. However, for the time being I just had to wait.

***

Later that night, as I lay in James' arms, thoughts of Gabrielle very much on my mind, I got up out of our bed and gathered up my jewellery box.

"James, Gabrielle gave me this as a birthday present, it belonged to her sister Alita. The night Jack took us to the shack in the woods, it was in Beth's car and when I prayed for help, the tune began to play; that's what frightened Jack, that and the fact the spirits filled the room with light."

James seemed relieved I was talking about it at last.

"Do you think, now you know Gabrielle is dead, she caused it to play?"

"Perhaps she did. What I can't understand is why I didn't know she was dead; why she has never shown herself to me."

"I can't answer that one darling, but there has been something bothering everyone at the nick: where did that bloody cricket bat come from?"

"If I tell you, please swear you'll not freak out."

"Ok, I swear."

"The spirit of Josh appeared and hit him with it."

"You're joking. He's not here now, is he, I mean he doesn't materialise when we're making love?"

"Josh saved me James; it's not a joke. It was the first time I had seen him since he died. I prayed and he saved me, end of story."

"Yes, I'm sorry, darling, if I sounded flippant." James took me once again in his arms. "Thank god he was there and Jack didn't actually … the bastard's an animal, I hope they throw away the key."

***

The high-pitched sound of the phone the next morning awoke us both from a deep slumber.

"Hello, yes, I'll just get her. Kate, it's Jeremy Daniels." James informed me as he passed me the receiver.

"Sorry to call you so early, Miss Oliver, but I've just remembered our conversation at dad's funeral. You said you had some photos, only we're leaving this afternoon to go back to Canada."

"Oh yes, of course, I'll bring them to you, where are you staying now?"

"We're at Lime House having a last look around the old place, it goes on the market tomorrow. We look forward to seeing you."

I had completely forgotten about the envelope: yes, there it was in the top drawer of my dressing table. Well, I thought, it has my name on it, so I think I must be entitled to at least a peek at the contents before handing it over to the brothers. Carefully, I slit open the top and was astonished to find it contained just one black-and-white photo, together with several pages of a letter.

"James, look at this: for some reason Doctor Daniels had written me a letter. I can't bear to read it, will you ... please?"

James propped himself up in bed. "So, who's in the picture?"

I turned it over to read the writing on the back.

"It's Doctor Daniels and my grandparents in the school playground, I hadn't realised they were friends." We stared at the old photo for several minutes, reminiscing about our time at the school, before James began to read.

Dear Kate,

This letter has been a long time coming, to my sorrow. Yesterday morning I received in the post what I can only describe as a poisoned pen letter, from an undisclosed source. It is to my shame that it has forced me into revealing secrets I have been required to keep over many years, secrets affecting so many people in so many ways.

"Shit, if we had known he had received a letter from the start, it would have saved a lot of heartache, and the police could have concentrated their investigations elsewhere."

"Let this be a lesson to you: always deal with correspondence immediately," James teased. I threw a pillow at him.

I have lived in and around Willow Green for most of my life; actually, I was in the same class in primary school as both your grandparents, Tom and Victoria. Tom and I were pals growing up, getting into all sorts of scraps as boys do, until the day my parents decided to send me away to private school. From there, I went to Queen Mary University London, where I studied medicine. Years later, I settled back into the village with my beautiful new wife Claire, by my side. Your grandfather had already bought Hill Farm, married Victoria, and had a son, Tom Junior, who he hoped would eventually take over the farm. Then, after years of trying, joyfully Claire found she was pregnant, and amazingly, so was Victoria. Life for us all was almost perfect – until gradually things began to fall apart.

Oh, how happy Tom and I were after the births of our sons. Sadly, Tom's joy did not last long – Tom Junior died suddenly from a brain tumour. I remember the day so vividly. I got a call from an hysterical Victoria saying he had collapsed at home, but when I got there it was too late, he was already dead. She was beside herself, your grandmother, and blamed me initially for not getting there quickly enough, crying I could have saved him – but no words were going to bring him back. Victoria retreated into herself – it was heart-breaking to witness. When she eventually died, I believe it was a relief to Tom, whose own health was also giving concern, being in the advance stages of rheumatoid arthritis.

Jonathan was really his saviour; he took the reins and ran the farm with great efficiency. When he married Rosemary, I thought at last life was on the up for Tom. Before I go any further, please remember Tom was my friend as well as my patient. The day I was called to the house, because he had had a fall, still makes me sick to my stomach.

Driving towards Hill Farm, I was sure I caught a glimpse of someone hiding in the hedgerow, but I put these thoughts to the back of my mind as I pulled up outside the house. To witness your best friend splayed unceremoniously on the floor, well, I know I am a doctor and have just about seen it all, but … he was my friend. Of course, your father was distraught, he implored me not to let Rosemary see his body, because of the baby she was carrying, which was actually the first time I learned Rosemary was pregnant.

"My grandfather lying on the ground was part of the scene I witnessed in my trance. Mother must have been pregnant with me. I had already thought I had been the cause of a shot gun wedding, so this just confirms it."

"She certainly wouldn't have been the first bride to walk down the aisle with a bun in the oven, that's for sure. Let's see what else he has to say."

I bent down to examine him but realised I was too late. The ambulance arrived about the same time as Rosemary, who looked flushed and upset. I happened to notice her dress was torn and there were several scratches on her arms. I pointed this out to her but she just dismissed me. On the way back, I stopped my car and had a look in the hedge where I thought I had seen someone. On a thorny branch, I found a small piece of material, the same material as her dress.

Because Tom had died unexpectedly at home, his body was taken away for an autopsy, which proved inconclusive about the cause of death. He had not had a heart attack or broken his neck; the coroner's judgment was, he had died of shock. I was not happy about the diagnosis so I made a request to see his body. I asked the coroner if he could have been smothered, in other words, had he been murdered? I recalled a discussion I had had previously with Tom, that he and Rosemary's relationship was a bit volatile, but was she capable of murder, I found myself asking? Nevertheless, the coroner was not interested in anything I had to say and was adamant his findings were correct.

"Christ, James, am I hearing right? Is mother a

serial killer; did she kill my grandfather as well?"

"Well, from what I've read so far, it seems Doctor Daniels thinks she did. Do you want me to go on, darling?"

"Yes, I need to know, please finish reading it."

Rosemary came to see me at the surgery that evening; she said she had heard I had been to see Tom's body, and did I know what had caused his death? I explained I was not at liberty to disclose any details because she was not the next of kin. She asked if I believed he had died unnaturally, which I thought was an odd question. Before she left, however, I enquired again about how she got her scratches, but she seemed agitated with my continued concern. It was then I reached into my drawer and withdrew the small piece of material I had found. Now she knew I suspected she had killed him. Rounding my desk, she leaned towards me and warned me if I said anything, she would say I had molested her, a scenario that is every doctor's nightmare. So began years of threats and bullying, I have to admit, I even feared for my own life.

"Poor man, what a monster mother is, how many more lives has she wrecked?"

Unfortunately, I have not told you the worst yet, Kate. Before your father married Rosemary, she told him she was pregnant; I think that was probably the reason he proposed. Perhaps she was expecting – I could never be sure – but there certainly was not any sign of a foetus when I examined her a week later at the clinic.

"What is Doctor Daniels trying to tell me, James? That mother was not pregnant with me before they got married, so obviously I was conceived after they got married, that's the norm isn't it?"

"If you'd let me get to the end of the letter Kate, perhaps we'll find out."

Now, I do not know if you have heard anything about your parents' past, but I have known your father, as I have said, since he was born. He has always been a bit of a lad as far as the women go, at least that is what I had understood from Tom.

On one particular day, a young girl who I immediately recognised as a worker from the farm came to see me – she was in such a bad state of mind I was quite concerned. In confidence, she told me she was pregnant with Jonathan's baby, but had been too frightened to tell him as he was now married – apparently they had been having a relationship before Jonathan had even met your mother. Unfortunately, as she left my surgery, Rosemary spotted her and demanded to know why she had been to see me. Evidently, she already had suspicions about the romance. I refused to tell her at first, but then the threats started again and, to my discredit, I relented and told her. Of course, she was furious, but then she asked how far into her pregnancy she was? I could see in her evil eyes a plan was hatching.

When she returned to the farm she confronted the girl and accused her of having an affair with Jonathan. She ordered her to leave without any explanation to your father and arranged for her to go into a home for unmarried mothers. In the meantime, to the outside world Rosemary's pregnancy was progressing; she even managed to fool Jonathan, giving a medical reason for not sleeping with him, until after the baby's birth, something she cajoled me into supporting.

Did I understand correctly, was Doctor Daniels telling me Rosemary was not my mother? The look on James' face showed deep concern, as he carried on reading the words that were gradually turning my world upside down.

Years later over a bottle of scotch, I had a moving conversation with your father. He believed Rosemary had tricked him into marriage, apparently there had been many times he had threatened to leave her for this girl; the love of his life, he called her. He had been devastated at her unexpected departure and never understood why she had left so abruptly. I knew, but I was too cowardly to say.

I was the doctor called in to attend the birth, such a dear little thing, cruelly snatched from her mother by a well-compensated nurse, as soon as she was born. The cries of that poor girl for her baby still haunt me to this very day. Rosemary tried to pay her for her silence of course, but she refused to take any money. I am sure by now, you have guessed, dear Kate, that the baby was you, and your mother was a beautiful French girl called Alita Duval.

I am so sorry to be relating such upsetting news in a letter, perhaps – if you can find it in your heart to forgive me – I know you must have so many questions, perhaps we can get together very soon.
Yours truly,
Doctor Daniels

James had hardly finished reading the words from a life extinguished, when I began to wail out in pain; not physical pain of course, but a deep emotional pain, only experienced when your heart is breaking into millions of pieces.

"No, please god, no, it can't be true? Alita was my mother, James hold me, it can't be true," and then a realisation dawned on me, "that means Gabrielle was my aunt, she must've come for me. Do you think mother found out, and that's why she killed her?"

CHAPTER 31 – A NEW IDENTITY

I was inconsolable. Rosemary Weston's sinful hands had destroyed the two most important human beings in my world: the two women who should still have been with me, sharing my life. She may not have physically murdered Alita, but her actions had certainly driven her to her grave. I would never be able to hold my real mother; never hear her voice, or feel the touch of her hand – there were not words strong enough to convey how I was feeling at this precise time about Rosemary Weston.

"Darling, I'm worried about you. I've called your father and Flo, and they're on their way. Look, Laura's here. Laura, Kate's had some more upsetting news, but I'll wait until everyone's arrived before I explain."

Although it was early in the day, Laura brought me up a very large brandy. Slowly, my flat started to fill with friends and family, all horrified at my demeanour. James began to read the correspondence that had caused me such pain. Not until he had finally folded the sheets of paper, which had contained disquieting words for everyone, did father draw me up to him, holding me close as he sobbed quietly on my shoulder, repeating how sorry he was, again and again.

"Are you still my sister, Kate? I couldn't bear it if you weren't."

"Of course she is, Ben." Beth answered as she

threw her arms around father and me. "If Alita was your mother, Kate, that means Madame Reiner is your grandmother, you're half French."

Gradually, with the medicinal effects of the brandy working in my system, I began to compose myself.

"Thank you all for coming round, I really appreciate the support. It has been quite an eventful few months for my whole family. So many long-held secrets have been revealed; you'll forgive me if it takes me some time to absorb the latest revelations, which I hope will be the last. Father, I would like to go to France for Gabrielle's funeral, would you go with me?" Father smiled weakly and nodded.

After everyone had left, James accompanied me to the police station so I could hand in Doctor Daniels' letter. Detective Sergeant Peters seemed very interested in the contents and promised to pursue the doctor's conviction that Rosemary Weston had murdered my grandfather, Tom Oliver. I asked if he could arrange a visiting order for me, so I could confront Rosemary face to face. He made a few phone calls and James and I were soon on our way to the prison.

***

To see 'mother' sitting behind a metal grill in handcuffs, well, what you sow you reap, I say.

"You're the last one I expected to see. Where's your brother and that puny wife of his? Tell him to come and visit me, I'd rather see him than you any day," she jeered.

I sat back in the chair and just stared at her for a while, absorbing her features. The greying roots just showing through her dyed auburn hair, those thin cruel lips encircling an acid tongue and those harrowing eyes, so full of hate for me. How thankful I was that we were not related.

"I'll tell Ben you would like to see him, he's a bit busy at the moment, but I'll ask him if he can spare some time. I've actually come to tell you this will be my one and only visit, Rosemary."

She stared at me with an intense glare. "I'm your mother, talk to me with some respect," she bellowed.

I drew closer to the grill. "I beg to differ. You're no mother of mine. My mother is in a grave in France, where you sent her, after you stole me from her."

"What the bloody hell are you on about?"

"Some evidence has come to light, Rosemary dear: Doctor Daniels wrote to me just before he died, the letter was right there in his study under your very nose. He told me everything and, of course, I felt obliged to pass on the information to the police. By the way, just so you know, Doctor Daniels wasn't the poisoned pen writer, so you had no reason to end his life. You're going to be in here for a very long time, you can't hurt me or anyone else anymore." I could see how she wanted to lunge at me, as she did when I was little. Enjoying her frustration, I continued my campaign: "Just answer me this, why did you kill my grandfather?"

I really did not expect a confession, so I was more than a little surprised when she bent forward and hissed quietly.

"He was a dirty old man, always barging in on me when I was dressing, with some lame excuse or another. Then he saw me strapping on the padding I wore under my maternity clothes, so I knew the game was up. It wasn't difficult, killing him; he was so weak and feeble. I shoved him down the stairs and then, while his eyes were still on me, I smothered him, just like I smothered Doctor Daniels and that slut of an au pair after she exposed herself to me as the sister of your whore of a mother, and you know I enjoyed every second of their agonising deaths." Beneath my controlled exterior, I was shaking; shaking with fury.

"That was all very interesting, I'm sure the police would like to hear your admission to all three murders."

She slumped back in her seat and roared with laughter. "I don't think so. Now go away I can't bear to look at you any longer."

Rising to leave, I had one more thing to say to her before I eradicated her from my life forever.

"Oh, by the way, you don't have to repeat what you've just told me: the police heard every word," I beamed triumphantly, patting the hidden recording device planted on me by Detective Sergeant Peters. With the sound of her screams echoing in my ears, I finally turned my back on Rosemary Weston and walked away.

***

The voyage to France became a family affair, including James, as everyone wanted to pay his or her respects. We planned to visit Madame Reiner with Emma as our interpreter, before the funeral, because I wanted to tell her personally who I was. We arrived after several hours of continued driving into the town of Montreuil where, surprisingly, Madame Reiner herself greeted us at her front door. Emma introduced our party in her impeccable French as Madame Reiner showed us into her front room.

"Emma, would you please tell Madame Reiner how sorry we are about Gabrielle." I insisted, smiling at Madame Reiner. Before Emma could repeat my words, Madame Reiner took both of my hands in hers.

"The first time I saw you, I thought you looked familiar, my dear."

"You speak English, but ..."

"Yes, I speak English, but when Gabrielle disappeared I swore I would not speak it again until she returned."

"Were you aware that Alita had an affair with my father and had had a baby in England, namely me?"

"No, I didn't know; if I had, I would have come for you. Apparently, Alita had confided in Gabrielle, that's how she knew where to find you. I only discovered in the last few weeks, from the British police, how my daughter had died, and about your existence from a private investigator." My grandmother tenderly wiped away the tears now trickling down my cheeks. "I hope you will be in my life for the rest of my days, my darling, it would mean so much to me."

I looked over at father for a sign of his acceptance before I replied; I did not want to hurt him any more.

"Of course, and you must come and visit us in England; father and I would love to show you around. Your husband, is he away?"

"No, he's left me for the cleaning lady."

With that startling disclosure, she rolled her head back and began to laugh heartily and, for some unexplained reason, we all joined in. And, you know something? It made us all feel so much better.

***

It was a crisp clear winter's morning as we gathered in the small church just outside Ardres. Grandmother had been so upset on seeing the state of the graveyard when she had visited a few days before that she had commissioned several gardeners to clear the area, so now it was a wonderful resting place for my mother, my aunt, and all the other departed souls.

Standing, looking down at the coffin being slowly lowered into its final resting place, I was suddenly aware of a presence close by. There she was, my spirit friend, between my grandmother and me. In a soft voice, she spoke to me for the very first time.

"Kate, welcome home, I'm so happy mother and you have found each other, take care my beautiful child, and always know I'm never far away."

The spirit of my mother rose above the congregation and then, to my great joy, a second apparition joined her. While I gazed upwards with overwhelming love in my heart, Alita and Gabrielle, hand in hand, disappeared into the ether.

EPILOGUE

With the lawns manicured to perfection and the borders filled with the perfume of roses and perennials of every hue, the gardens at Lime House looked magnificent in the summer sunshine.

"Our guests are arriving darling, I don't mean to rush you ..." James called out from the bottom of the stairs.

"Ok, I'll be down in a minute."

I still could not believe our luck in buying Lime House. It had been on the market for over two years before we moved in. The roof was leaking and the plaster was beginning to peel from the walls and ceilings, but none of these problems was insurmountable. However, nobody, it seemed, wanted to buy a house where a murder had taken place – but ghosts did not bother my family.

I married James, soon after Rosemary had been given three life sentences: an acceptable result for three lost lives. Father had looked extremely proud as he walked me up the floral aisle in Willow Green church, with Beth in close attendance as my maid of honour. James might not have been my first love, but he is certainly my last.

Months later, grandmamma (the name my French grandmother wants me to call her) who is now a regular visitor to our shores, insisted on buying us something more suitable for our growing family. For, to our delight, we found out I was pregnant with twins and quite honestly, a one-bedroomed flat would have been more than a bit of a squeeze. Even though we protested it was too much, grandmamma bought Lime House for us because, as she insisted, she wanted somewhere comfortable to stay when she visited and I could consider it part of my inheritance.

Everyone we knew had been invited to our very first garden party. Mrs. Barbara Hamilton was quick to corner me in the refreshment tent.

"I must say Kate, you have made so many improvements in such a short time, what's your secret, my dear?"

"Well, Barbara, we found a really good handyman, I certainly can recommend him if you want his number. I've been told the garden looks as good as it did when Flo's late husband Harold used to attend it. Didn't he used to do the odd job for you?"

"Um ... yes, he did, thank you dear, but I'm thinking of selling Manor House and moving into something smaller, since ... well you might as well hear it from me, since Mr. Hamilton moved out and, of course, you know it will be a long time before my son Stephen comes home."

I certainly did. The police had found his fingerprints on Harold's spanner, although unfortunately their discovery was not enough evidence for the courts. However, he had finally been sent away, for a very long stretch, when the vile excuse for a human being was found guilty of two counts of rape.

"Kate," called out Flo, "come and join us."

My very good friends, the original members of the 'The Ladies Book Club' – Flo, Laura, Brenda and Emily – were enjoying the hog roast, the aroma of which was filling the air.

"This is wonderful, Kate, can I get you a plate?"

"No thanks Flo, perhaps a bit later. Ursula, it's lovely to see you, how are you feeling?"

Ursula, now sadly confined to a wheelchair, still insisted on attending our meetings as often as her health allowed.

"I'm feeling quite good actually. It seems such a lifetime ago since you first crashed our circle, you have certainly blossomed into a beautiful mother, Kate. Where are the children, by the way?"

Blushing from her compliment, I pointed towards the bouncy castle.

"They've been playing with their cousin Christopher since Ben inflated it early this morning, hopefully they'll all sleep well tonight. Please excuse me, I must go and find James."

There he was, my handsome husband, playing boules with my father and grandmamma.

"Can I borrow him for a minute?" I smiled, guiding him away to the doorway at the side of the house.

"I was winning, darling, what's the matter?"

"Does a wife need an excuse to want a kiss from her husband, without anything being wrong?" I looked deep into his eyes. "I am so happy James, sometimes it frightens me that I'll wake up one day and it's all been a dream."

We stood together, locked in an embrace, until the sound of Beth's voice put an end to our amour.

"Gabrielle's had a bit of an accident I'm afraid, I think Alita managed to push her into the only puddle on the driveway."

"No, I didn't, she fell. Mummy, are you cross with

me?" I gathered my daughters up into my arms.

"Girls, mummy's not cross, it's only mud; it'll wash out. Come on, let's go and get something to eat, I'm starving."

THANK YOU!

To my Reader:

Many thanks for buying *A Troubled Soul*, I hope you enjoyed reading it.

If you did enjoy it, please post a review at Goodreads or your favourite social network site and let your friends know about *A Troubled Soul*.

Don't forget to read the first in the series – *All For the Love of Josie*, if you haven't already.

Look out for more stories from *Willow Green* coming soon.

Happy Reading!
All the best
Evelyn

CONTACT DETAILS

Like on Facebook: facebook.com/1evelynharrison

Cover designed by: www.StunningBookCovers.com

Published by: Raven Crest Books
www.ravencrestbooks.com

Follow us on Twitter:
www.twitter.com/lyons_dave

Lightning Source UK Ltd.
Milton Keynes UK
UKOW02f1055010715

254399UK00007B/81/P